# The Triplets and The Blonde

## A BILLIONAIRE ROMANCE

### CALLIE SKY

*The Triplets and The Blonde*

Copyright (c) 2023 by Callie Sky

For more information contact:

authorcalliesky@gmail.com

Cover design by: Cat Cover Design

*To my husband John because you have a sexy butt.*

# Trigger Warnings –
## These may contain spoilers

If any of these are a trigger for you don't read this book. There are so many other amazing books out there. No book is worth it.

Kidnapping

Violence

Death

Homelessness

Throat grabbing

Pregnancy

Sex scenes

Sex scenes with multiple partners

Stabbing

Prostitution

Starvation

Death Threats

Loss of Mother

## CHAPTER 1

# *Kira and the deal*

I LICKED THE CREAMY DOUGHNUT FROSTING FROM my finger. A cupcake would have been more appropriate, but doughnuts were harder to come by. And I was all for items that were difficult to acquire.

The wax on the candle melted causing it to droop. The flame flickered, threatening to extinguish. I closed my eyes debating on my wish.

My mothers voice swam in my head, *People like us don't wish. Kira, this is your life and all it will ever be.* She never dreamed of a better life, not that it would have done her any good. The homeless had two choices; Stay invisible or die. She chose the latter. That was five years ago and her voice still played in my head.

When I opened my eyes to blow out my candle the flame had burnt some of the frosting. Wax had melted all over. Concentrating, I shut my eyes again. *I wish life wasn't like this.* It wasn't much of a wish for my twenty second birthday, but it was the same one I had always made.

As I blew out the candle I saw Vickie in my peripheral vision. Her thick hair was done in long braids down her back.

As she barreled toward me a few braids fell to frame her tiny face. If pixies were real, she would be their leader. Everything about her was small, even her voice. I had tried to teach her to have a commanding voice when she meant business. It led to fits of laughter.

She stopped in front of my dumpster and wrinkled her button nose. With the temperatures rising above the nineties, the garbage was extra ripe. She sat down on the crate next to me and took the doughnut from my hand. After ripping it in half she handed me back part of it.

"Happy Birthday." She took a bite letting out a low moan. "How do you always pilfer the best desserts?"

"It's what I do." I winked at her and shoved my whole piece into my mouth, melted wax and all.

Ever since I lost my mom, I had to find a way to survive. I took her advice about being invisible as literally as possible. It helped me hone my skills as being the go to person on the streets. If you needed something, I could get it, for a price.

"Oh," her tiny voice squeaked. "I rushed over because someone is looking for you."

I shrugged. The food was all stuck in my teeth and roof of my mouth preventing me from talking. People were always looking for me. My particular services were hard to come by. Vickie's on the other hand weren't, but I wasn't one to judge.

I realized he was out of place the second he stopped in front of me. With my right hand I shielded the sun from my eyes to further inspect him. His long brown trench coat covered most of his very expensive designer gray suit. The shine on his shoes was enough to blind someone. Everything about him screamed, *I'm rich.*

Don't get me wrong, we get people with money in Poor Town. They show up, pay for services that people like Vickie provided and go back to their perfect lives. My services were useless to someone like him. He obviously had everything he needed.

"Are you Kira the finder?" He squatted down and got eye level with me. Everything about the look in his eyes said he was studying me and I was not what he expected.

"Yea, The Finder. If you are looking for other services, Vickie can help. I don't hook." I nodded my head toward Vickie.

The man's eyes never left my face. Men were always thinking they could intimidate women. Not me. I had never been and never would be afraid of anyone. Living on the streets hardened a person. Something this guy knew nothing about.

"Back up. You're in my space," I snapped.

Vickie's hand jetted out to grab mine. The streets never toughened her. Having been in bed with so many men and women, I had thought she wouldn't have been scared of them. She was. Then again, maybe that was why. She had told me stories of people's kinks in bed. I wasn't downing anyone's kink, but some were so violent she would turn down a potential client.

"I need you to collect something for me." The man stood and took a step back, giving me my space.

"What could she get you that you don't have?" Vickie whispered, her voice even lower than normal.

"If I could speak with you in private, Miss Kira." He looked around as if he was going to find an office.

I squeezed Vickie's hand and released it. Nodding my head toward the end of the alley, letting her know it was okay for her to leave. She got up and walked a few feet away, out of earshot, but close enough if I needed her.

"So, what can I get you that you can't buy yourself?" I stood and stared him in the eyes. I was letting him know I wasn't afraid.

He handed me a business card. On the front was a bunch of squiggly lines and the name Carlos Garcia. I knew that name, but I couldn't place it. I flipped it over, on the back was written *10pm Garcia Corp. Come Alone.*

I laughed.

He had started to walk away, as if the card was enough to entice me. When I started laughing, he turned and came back over. "What do you find so funny Miss Kira?"

"Gee, I don't know. Maybe the fact that you, Carlos, think I'm gonna meet you late at night at some building across town." I took the card and shoved it into his hand.

"Miss Kira, I would rather not discuss such matters here." The disgust on his face could have been seen across miles.

"Well, if you want my services, this is where we talk. If not, find one of your rich peeps to do your dirty work," I snapped.

Dealing with The Rich was always risky business. I normally didn't do it. Not that I was against it, but they expected us to do a lot for very little cash. And I never, not once, had one of The Elite in front of me actually speaking to me. We had three classes; Homeless, Rich, and Elite. My mother once told me that's not how it always was.

My mother had told me there was a thing called the middle class. Average people that didn't have tons of money. They had houses, cars, and usually didn't beg for food. Then the poor got poorer and became the homeless. Millions of people out on the streets like it was nothing.

The middle class vanished. The Rich took over, living in mansions, and then there was the Elite. Well, they ruled everything. My mom showed me books about a thing called 'the government.' It was as much a fantasy as the stories I read. Elite's were in charge. Meaning one thing: Money controlled everything.

"Miss Kira, if you insist. I need you to retrieve a bag for me. If you accept, I will give you all the details." Again his eyes darted around. That's when I realized he was nervous. His kind didn't go down dark alleys, to talk to filthy homeless people. He was hoping he would have already been gone, and we would have this meeting in his part of town. A place safe for someone like him, an Elite.

"Carlos, let me be super clear. You tell me everything I need to know to retrieve this bag. If I can do it, you pay half now. Depending on how hard this is gonna be will depend on how long it will take me." I crossed my arms over my chest to show him I was tired of his back and forth.

"Fine." He ran his hand through his hair and mumbled something to himself. Then to me he said, "The bag is behind a painting at 44 Cartright Ave. I need it by midnight tomorrow. I will meet you here. Before you ask, I'm not sure which painting. Probably the Van Gough, knowing them."

"No." I shook my head and sat back down.

"No? Rumors claim you are the best." Carlos practically stomped his foot.

There was The Elite's and then there were the Cartrights. So rich they named the street after themselves. "You are asking me to steal from the family that owns half of New Boston. Are you crazy?"

Anyone that lived in or near New Boston knew the Cartrights. The family expanded across the ten countries within the United States, but this town was their birth place. My mom told me when the economy shifted they helped drive people from their homes. They were ruthless, evil, and killed without remorse. No way was I going near their mansion.

He looked up and down the alley, again. Then he squatted close to me. Reaching into his pocket he pulled out a thick white envelope. "I'm asking you to steal one last time, to change your life around. Do you really want to live like this forever?" He handed me the envelope.

I knew I shouldn't open it. Every atom of my being told

me to give it back. Walk away. I gripped the envelope. It was stuffed full of cash, it had to be. I opened it.

My eyes bugged out of my head. My heart pounded in my chest. Sweat dripped down my temples. It was. It was. I just couldn't believe it. I made a weird gurgle noise every time I tried to speak. Suddenly, I was very aware of Vickie watching us. That was enough to change both of our lives. She would never have to hook again.

"Fifty thousand now. A hundred thousand more tomorrow at midnight," he whispered. Then he got up and walked away.

I shoved the money into my bookbag. Stealing from the Cartrights was suicide. It was nuts just to consider it, but with that kind of money I could change mine and Vickie's lives. Could I really walk away from that kind of cash?

"Okay, fill me in." Vickie plopped beside me.

"Would you come with me? Go to Mexico, start over." I grabbed her hands to show her how serious I was.

"Mexico?" she whispered as if the word alone would get us in trouble.

Mexico was a dreamland. There were no homeless people, no Elite, no rulers. They apparently still had a government and housing for everyone. It was where all of us dreamed of, but to get there cost money. Lots of money.

"Yes, Mexico. You would never have to hook again. I would never have to steal. Imagine it. We could have a life, find love, start a family." I waved my hand in the air like she could see the words I spoke.

"You know how much money that costs? Not to mention it's four countries to cross, each harder to pass than the one before. Even if we get that far, how do you plan on getting past the wall into Mexico?" She shook her head. When we were little we dreamed of this. I could have made this happen and she was being skeptical.

6

"This job could make our dreams come true. It's a hundred and fifty k." I knew it was dangerous, but it was worth the risk.

"What's the job? Maybe I could help." She knew there was no way we could turn this down.

"Robbing the Cartrights," I whispered.

"What you're gonna steal from The Triplets?" She grabbed my arms, her nails dug into my skin.

CHAPTER 2

*Kira and the painting*

THE MANSION WAS SO TALL AND WIDE, I COULDN'T see where it ended. It was easily as big as three blocks. 44 Cartright Ave was bigger than some small towns. The stonework had intricate patterns and appeared to be in mint condition. All the lights were off and from what I could tell there were no cars in the driveway. Which happened to run the length of the entire house.

Most people assumed breaking into a house at night was the best time. It wasn't. The owners were usually gone during the day. With the right outfit, I could waltz into the service entrance and no one would question me.

I had to use some of the money Carlos gave me to clean up. Luckily, I knew the guy who ran the gym around the corner. After a lot of soap and scrubbing, I stopped smelling like a dumpster.

The uniform was hard to get. The Elite employed people to do everything they didn't want to. As if that wasn't humiliating enough they made them wear uniforms while they scrubbed toilets and cooked meals. The Cartrights had their employees wear yellow shorts, white knee high socks, and black polo's. I looked like an oversized bumble bee.

Sneaking into the service entrance was easy. It was unlocked and not a soul was around. For a brief moment I thought I could actually pull this off. I turned the corner and saw a man sauntering toward me.

He wore the same outfit as me and had short red hair perfectly parted down the middle. He was fit, but not the pumping iron kind. He appeared like he had way too much energy and didn't need to drink coffee.

"Sweetie," he called down the hall toward me.

I took a deep breath and walked right at him. He was either going to think I was new or kick me out. If it was the latter I would have to find a different way in. Yea, I should have pretended not to hear him and walk away. Had I, that would have set off more alarms with him.

"Sweetie." He linked his arm in mine as if we were old friends. I immediately liked him. "Did you read the whole welcome packet? The Trips like women to have their hair parted down the middle in pigtails. Unless of course it inter-feres with religion. Ya know hijabs or other head coverings."

There were so many things he said that confused me. I knew a few people that worked for Elite's and never did they mention a 'welcome packet.' This guy was making it sound like it was a good thing to work for them. Pigtail hair require-ments? I didn't even know what to think of that. "I didn't get a chance to read the packet. The Trips?"

"The Triplets: Aiden, Derek, and Jason. They really are great to work for. You are gonna love them. Well maybe not Aiden, but he is just rough on the outside." He rambled on as he led me down hall after hall.

Every wall was covered in paintings. One of them had to be hiding the bag. I just didn't have a clue on how I was going to find the right one. I didn't even know what a Vango looked like or if I was saying it right.

Men and women walked down the halls doing various jobs. Some cleaned, others carried trays of food or gardening tools. A short stocky woman wrestled a pig that was on a leash. Man, I hoped that wasn't going to be dinner. Each servant wore that same uniform and all had their hair in pigtails or if their hair was short, it was parted down the middle. Except a few that had on hijabs. The pigtails was such an odd hairstyle choice.

"So, what will I be doing?" I asked hoping that wasn't something I was supposed to know.

"Not sure. That's not up to me. But if I could guess I would say maid duty. They love to watch the pretty girls clean." He stopped in front of a door that was slightly ajar. "If they have you cleaning their rooms you're a shoe in for a night with them."

"Huh?" A night with them would never happen and why did he say them as if more than one of the triplets would be involved? Not that it mattered, I wasn't into that sort of thing no matter how many were or weren't involved.

"Have you not heard the rumors? They share everything. Imagine three men tending to your every desire." He placed his hands over his heart as if he had imagined it, a lot.

I had no desire for any of that. I shook my head, I was getting distracted. I had to find the bag and get out. Before I could open my mouth to ask about the Vango painting, he pushed the door open.

"I was talking so much I forgot to ask your name," he said.

"Oh, uh Kira." I should have given a fake name. Normally I would have, but the man in the room had distracted me.

He stood behind a wide wood desk with multiple computer screens. His white button up shirt was open, exposing a perfectly sculpted chest with enough hair to add texture. I wanted to run my fingers down his happy trail. His black dress pants hung low showing off his abs. He was sex appeal in human form. I wanted to feel the scruff on his face across my back.

That man was what stories were written about. He was the lead in every woman's fantasy. I couldn't stop staring at him and I instantly hated him for it.

"Kira, Sweetie, are you listening? Have a seat and Mr. Cartright will be with you shortly." He gave me a quick hug. "If you need anything, I'm Pat."

I should have left. They would just say I must have gotten scared and quit. Going during the day was to avoid owners, not meet them. Once they realized something was stolen, they would know it was me. The Triplets would make the connection between the new girl and the missing bag. Not to mention, he would realize he didn't hire me.

Watching him talk on his cell phone, in his office, in his big ass mansion, angered me. Instead of helping the homeless he worried about his servants wearing pigtails and sharing the women with his brothers like they were objects.

"Come in," he ordered without even looking up at me.

I stepped inside, but refused to sit down like Pat had told me to do.

For ten minutes I stood there. Ten minutes. He stayed on the phone discussing some upcoming party. Not once during that time did he look at me. A few times I even stuck out my tongue at him. Still nothing.

"Sit," he demanded.

I stood.

"Do you need some hair ties?" He swept his hand into his pocket. His shirt exposed more of his sculpted skin.

I sucked in a deep breath. "No."

"My brother Derek must have hired you as a joke." He ran his hand through his dark brown hair. "I don't like defiant."

"I don't like being told how to wear my hair and to sit like an animal." I clenched my teeth, getting this far and being tossed out now would make stealing from this house more difficult.

He walked around his desk and approached me. Inches from me I could smell his citrus cologne. He looked me up and down, stopping at my lips and licking his in turn. A shiver ran up my spine.

"Go clean something." He waved his hand toward the door, clearly dismissing me.

I turned and that's when I saw it. A painting of swirls. Blues, yellows and whites danced around. It was of the sky but so much more. Art wasn't too common on the streets. There were a few guys that would draw your portrait for a few bucks. But color. Color wasn't easy to get. Paint and brushes were for the Rich. Most paintings I had seen were boring. But this one moved. This one was full of life.

"It's my favorite," the asshole said.

I jumped, having forgotten he was there.

"I didn't think someone like you could appreciate art." He came to stand next to me.

"We can appreciate it, we just don't have the money to waste." I turned to him. "Ya know 'cause we spend our money on food."

For a brief second the corner of his mouth twitched. "Good point. Most of the Van Goughs were destroyed in a fire. This one is an original and cost a fortune."

My jaw dropped. This was 'the painting.' It had to be. I was so close to it. There was no way I could overpower this man and get behind the painting. Sighing, I realized I would have to come back. Hopefully this asshole didn't stay in his office all the time.

I spent the next few hours mapping out the mansion. Exits, quick escapes, places where people congregated and where they didn't. Pat found me inspecting a window down the hall from Mr. Asshole Cartright's office. I lifted the window a few inches so I could get out fast if needed.

"Sweetie, jumping ship already?" Pat asked.

I grabbed at my chest. I hadn't even heard him saunter over. "I, um, needed fresh air."

"What job did Aiden give you?" Pat linked his arm into mine.

"He ordered me to go clean something," I sighed.

"You got him so frazzled he couldn't properly assign you. I love it." Pat fake fanned himself. "Okay Sweetie, let's give you the grand tour."

Sixty-three! That's how many bedrooms there were. Unless you included the servants' wing that bumped the number up to seventy-seven. Only fourteen of the hundred servants actually lived on the property. The rest were still homeless. The Cartrights allowed them to come in early and shower. Gee, how nice.

Along with all the bedrooms there were twenty nine bathrooms, six kitchens, ten living rooms, and other various rooms. Some had purpose, others were empty and useless.

We walked past a door with two deadbolts. According to Pat, The Trips used that as their 'sharing room.' He did air quotes on the end part. Unless they invited you, that room was off limits. Even if they begged me, I would never go in there. Never.

On the third floor was the room of all rooms. My mouth dropped as I stared at the biggest library I had ever seen. Floor to ceiling shelves. Multiple ladders stretched along the walls. I read a book once about a girl trapped in a castle. The beast had a library and let her read all day. For a brief moment I wished I was her. This place could have been my castle.

Across the room were glass cases. Inside were so many books I had never heard of. Unhinged Witch, Butterflies on my Window, Romeo and Juliet, 22 Saints. I ran my fingers along the glass.

"Banned books. Jason collects them," Pat said. When I gave him a quizzical look he kept talking. "Jason is one of The Trips. He has a love of books. Spends most of his time reading."

"It's beautiful." I wanted to stay. I could keep my job here and read in my free time. They would probably never realize I wasn't an actual hire. Sighing I realized that wasn't possible. I had to help Vickie.

"The linen closet is down the hall. Let's get you some supplies and then you can clean in here." Pat turned and led me to the closet. It was bigger than the alley I lived in. A family of six could have lived in there. Pat grabbed some dust rugs and a spray bottle. When I asked about the broom and mop, he laughed. Someone else did that every night.

Pat left me alone for a few hours. Instead of cleaning I curled up on a comfy leather sofa and read. This was bliss. Never in my life had I been so relaxed. Even knowing what I had to do, I fell into the story. The sun began to set in the window next to me. There was only a few hours before midnight.

"I never understood why those books were banned. That one is about a witch in The Bermuda Triangle." Aiden walked toward me. His words were calming but his walk still had his cocky arrogance.

"I was just taking a peak." I closed the book. "I'll get back to cleaning, not that it needs it."

"No worries. I'm Jason and you must be new. Not many of your people read." Jason Cartright stuck out his hand for me to shake.

"My people aren't afforded the same opportunities as someone like you." I pushed past him and fled down the hall.

Jason was identical to his brother except he seemed to not

be such an arrogant asshole. Although his comment about 'your people' was ridiculous.

Pushing aside thoughts of Jason's scruff between my thighs, I searched for Aiden's office. My memory was pretty good when it came to directions. Of course I wasn't normally searching through mansions. After wandering for almost an hour, I saw the door with the two deadbolts. It was slightly ajar. The moans flowed through the air. *Turn around, KIra. Get the bag and get out.*

Is that what I did? No! I stood there listening to a woman's cries of ecstasy. Then she gagged as if she couldn't breathe. I pushed open the door because clearly the woman was in trouble. That asshole Aiden had to be hurting her.

They didn't hear the door open. One of The Trips was laying on the sofa, butt naked. A woman in just pigtails was bent over him bobbing up and down. She would slowly lick and then suck hard causing the gagging sound. The man let out a heartfelt laughter as he grabbed her pigtails. He looked like he had never been so happy. From the gleam in his eye I could tell he was the third brother, Derek, the other two seemed too serious.

With each laugh the woman got deeper on his dick. Behind her was another of The Trips. He slid his cock in and out of her. A sheen of sweat covered his back. He had kept his black slacks on. Jason had been wearing jeans and a t-shirt. So, unless he changed, I was watching Aiden have sex. I tried to control my body, but it betrayed me. The more I watched the wetter I got. I wanted to slide my hand into my shorts and relieve the pressure.

I shouldn't have been so turned on by this. The woman was being used as a one time thing by these men. Yet, she was more than willing. One of the men I hadn't met yet, so I couldn't say much about him. But the other was a complete asshole. He tossed me out of his office and here I was watching him have sex. The realization practically slapped me across the face. *He was in here. That meant his office was empty.*

Praying that they hadn't noticed the bumble bee in the doorway, a seriously awful uniform, I turned on my heels. Forcing myself to walk slowly, I headed to his office. Visions of what I had just witnessed played in my head. I had never had sex, I mean one day I was going to and part of me wanted it to be like that. Two men filling my needs. Well, maybe three men.

Did Jason ever join them? Was he too busy to partake or did he not share like his brothers?

"Sweetie," Pat called down the hall. He waved his hand in the air as if I didn't see him.

I didn't have time for his chatter. Aiden could finish at any time. Pat waved again. I sighed and approached him. "Yes?"

"You really stuck to your gun on the whole hair thing, love it. So anyway, we do a big dinner. Like so much food. You can eat as much as you want. It's in the dining hall in the basement." He linked his arm in mine. "I could walk you."

Never in my life had I eaten as much as I wanted. Yea, I could find whatever food I wanted, but eating too much left less for others. There were way too many people starving on the streets to be so careless. It made me hate The Trips even more.

"I shouldn't be surprised that they waste food," I half muttered to myself.

"Waste? Sweetie, nothing gets tossed. We get to take leftovers back to our family's. Then at least twice a week they donate anything that might not be used. Part of the reason New Boston isn't as bad as other places is because of The Trips." Pat started guiding me down the staircase.

My heart fluttered. I had known that our homeless population wasn't as bad as other cities. Shit, it was part of the reason why I stuck around. No way did any Elite have anything to do with that. *Ha, I guess I was wrong.*

I could have stayed and worked for The Cartrights. Bring food to Vickie. Life could have remained as it was, only slightly better. I could have a real job instead of being a thief. I would no longer be Kira the Finder. But then what? Still live on the streets? Vickie would still hook. In Mexico we would be free. We would have a place of our own, a life not dictated by our current economic status.

I sighed and pulled my arm from Pat's. He turned to me and scrunched up his face. "I'll meet you there. I forgot something." Turning from him I fled back toward the office. A piece of me broke knowing I lied to him. He had been kind to me and I used him.

*Focus!*

Luckily, the office was still empty. Aiden must have been dripping with sweat by now. I shook my head, that didn't matter.

The painting that mesmerized me earlier still had the same effect. I had to stand on my tip toes to unhook it from the wall. Just like Carlos said, it covered the bag. The problem was so did a safe in the wall. At least I assumed the bag was in there.

Earlier that morning I went to visit a guy that runs a shop on 5th street. Total underground stuff. He hired me a lot in the past to get stuff for him. Two years prior he paid me to break into a lab and steal a few items. It was how I knew what I needed. Granted I could have gone right to the lab and got it from there, but there was no time for that.

Guy charged me five grand, which was nuts because I was the reason he had it. Staring at the safe, I was glad I paid the money.

Removing the tin box from my bra, I peeled back the seal. Hundreds of nanos lay dormant inside. I removed the pen from the lid. After drawing a circle around the lock, I clicked the pen on.

The tiny bots, no bigger than a push pin, jumped out of the box and attacked the lock. They were acid nanos. I wasn't sure about the science behind it. I knew they disintegrated anything the ink from the pen had enclosed, but that was it.

The bots emitted a humming sound as they went to work. Dust flew into the air. I bounced from heel to heel, willing it to hurry up. I felt like I was standing in front of Aiden again and he was ignoring me. The bots took their time, just like he did.

After what felt like hours, but was probably only five minutes the little machines busted through the safe. I clicked the pen and they dropped like sand bugs.

Footsteps.

Shit.

I grabbed the bag and left the nanos. Which sucked because I could have sold them back to Guy for half the price.

Leaving the office I caught a glimpse of Aiden. Shirtless and still wearing his slacks. He must have just finished up or he had an alarm on his safe. I had a feeling it was the latter.

"Stop," he commanded.

Fuck that! I took off toward the open window. His footsteps didn't hasten, at least it didn't sound like it. I grabbed the window and tossed it open. Not wanting to take any chances I swung myself out the window, practically head first. Stupid, I know. I panicked.

The window was close to the ground and I was able to grab onto a bush to soften the blow. A hand wrapped around my ankle.

Fuck!

## CHAPTER 3
### *Kira and the escape*

I yanked my leg. Nothing. He wasn't giving up. Granted I didn't blame him. I did just steal from him. Not that he needed whatever was in the bag. But I needed the money the bounty brought.

My fingers were slipping from the bush. Aiden was pulling me back into the window. *Nope, not gonna happen.*

When I was twelve, I started acquiring items for other people. It was good cash and my tiny body fit into places others couldn't. Shortly after I lost my mother, I was caught by a man named Tang. The man strung me by my ankles until I confessed to being paid to steal his jewelry.

Instead of being mad, Tang taught me to be better. Lesson one was to use my core to pull myself up. The reason for that was to never stay too long in a compromising position.

I twisted my body so I could see Aiden. He smiled down at me. He seemed to be enjoying that he had caught me. *Not for long, Buddy.*

Using my core I did an incline sit up to become face to face with Aiden. If he was shocked he didn't show it. Before I could get lost in his dreamy eyes, I slammed my head into his nose. Head wounds bleed a lot and fast. His nose proved that as blood splattered on my face as well as his.

He screamed and stumbled back, releasing my ankle. I fell backward into the bushes. Way too many pricklers bore into my back and side. *Fuck.*

"You are gonna be punished for that!" Aiden growled.

I scrambled and crawled out of the bush. Once my feet were firmly on the ground, I ran.

"I will find you!" Aiden screamed. It sounded like he gurgled on blood, but I wasn't looking back to see. He would be fine. The Elite had people that could mend a broken nose in minutes, at least that was the rumor.

That was another reason I hated The Elite. Every time I had a broken bone, and there were plenty of times, I had to wait for them to heal. I was pretty sure one of my rib bones never did heal.

Tang, the man who taught me to be a better thief, asked me to steal a book for him. It was a first edition Death Divides Us, so yea I understood the appeal. It was one of the only fantasy books not on the ban list so it was very popular. A first edition was priceless.

The owner had booby-trapped his basement. *Who even does that?* Well, one trap door got me and broke a few fingers along with a rib. I got out with the book, thank you very much. As a reward Tang gave me a week off and fresh strawberries. I showed up the next day refusing to take time off from training.

That was why I was the best. Years of training would pay off with this one score. If I could get away. Aiden had to have alerted his security. People were running at me and shouting. A metal fence started popping up from the far end of the property. According to my research, I had fifty-five seconds to make it before there was no escape.

Ignoring the pain in my back, I ran. Jumping over a puppy

that was taking a nap in the grass, I pushed forward with everything I had. More of the fence locked into place, getting closer. If they caught me, nope, I would not think of that.

They wouldn't catch me, I was too good. I ran. Pumping my legs faster I gave it everything I had. My foot connected with metal. The ground shook. For a brief moment I was suspended in the air. Using the momentum I flung myself forward. My face slammed into the ground. Shit, that stung. I had caught the fence as it was springing up.

I rolled onto my back to see the fence I was just on, clicking into place. It was electrified which was why the security skidded to a halt. I was free. The Trips stormed out of their mansion. Aiden had his hand still covering his face. Served him right.

After flipping them the middle finger, I turned and took off. It looked like all the security was on the other side of the fence, but I wasn't taking any chances. I ran.

My alley was miles away. Even though I was good at running, I wasn't one that did it for fun. Stopping to catch my breath I leaned against a wall. A few guys whistled at me as they walked by. Creeps.

I rolled my eyes and started walking again. It would be dark soon, which meant midnight was closing in. Soon, I would hand over the bag and I would have enough money for me and Vickie to get to safety.

Sticking to the walls and shadows I made it home in about an hour. A few of the other people in the alley gave me questionable looks. I ignored them all. It wasn't the first time I came home in an odd outfit. At least I didn't have my hair in pigtails.

Once I was at my spot I moved the dumpster forward to block me. I draped a sheet from the brick wall to the dumpster. Now fully blocked I pulled out my bookbag and changed into sweatpants and a hoodie. A t-shirt and bra were out of the question. My back was still in pain from the bushes. Vickie would bandage me up when she came by later.

I took the bag and hid it behind a brick that I had loosened years ago. Until Carlos gave me the money it would stay there. No way would he get the product before I got my money.

"Hey, you home?" Vickie asked on the other side of the sheet.

"Right on time. I need some patching up." I pulled the sheet down.

"I figured." She lifted a small green bag. It was her first aid kit. She kept it stocked. At times both of our jobs were dangerous.

A few years ago, I had to bandage her up from a violent customer. It took her weeks to recover. That was part of the reason this bounty meant so much to me. Never again would she come home bleeding from a guy that couldn't control himself. Never again would she be in pain.

"How did it go?" She sat on the milk crate waiting for me.

"That sounded like doubt?" I sat on the ground in front of her and lifted the hoodie to expose my back.

"No doubt. But geez, Kira, this is bad. Did they catch you?" She poured alcohol on the wounds. "I'm gonna have to pick out all these thorns."

"Fuck, that stings. No one can catch me." I ground my teeth.

Barney came running toward us. He was an older man that normally kept to himself. I would give him food when I had extra. Never once had I seen him run, I didn't know he could. His jacket swayed behind him as he got closer.

"What's wrong?" Vickie stood, spilling more alcohol on my back. Shit, that hurt.

"Kira, you gotta go. Some people are looking for you. One has blood dripping down his face. They look pissed." Barney looked behind him. "I can distract them for a bit, but you gotta go."

*Fuck! How the heck did they find me?* New Boston was huge. It took them no time at all to find me. I may have slightly underestimated them. I pulled down my hoodie and grabbed my bookbag. "Thank you Barney, go, don't get involved."

Barney turned and took off down the alley.

"Kira, you gotta run." Vickie grabbed my arm.

"Listen. This has everything. It should be enough to get you to Mexico. Don't look at me like that. Here, hide in the dumpster." I linked my hands together to give her a boost.

"No, I'm not leaving you." Vickie wrapped her arms around me.

"I don't have time for this. If anything happens to you, then none of this would have been worth it." I pushed her off of me and grabbed her foot to push her into the dumpster with my bookbag. It had the money in there from Carlos that he had already given me. It would have been easier to get to Mexico with the rest, but now there was no time. "I'll break free and meet you in Mexico."

She shook her head as tears streamed down her face.

"Please. I'll never forgive you if you don't hide." A low blow, yes, but I had to make sure she was okay.

Vickie finally listened and climbed into the dumpster. I pushed it back against the wall and shut the lid. Sitting back down on the milk crate I waited. There was a slight chance they would keep walking. Maybe they would think I was just another homeless person. Yes, I could have hid in the dumpster with Vickie, but I didn't want to risk it.

I didn't know what was in the bag I stole. It didn't matter to me. If The Trips were desperate for it, they would start searching dumpsters, and I would give myself up before they found Vickie.

A woman that was new to the alley came sauntering down. Behind her was The Trips. Aiden kept wiping his nose. Ha, I did a number on him. I ducked my head.

That bitch stopped right in front of my milk crate. I saw her feet but I refused to look up. I should have ran. The woman didn't really know me, maybe she would lead them past me.

"This is her. Can I have my money now?" the woman asked.

Shit. I jumped up and pushed into the woman. She stumbled backward crashing into the men. I took off running, at least they wouldn't find Vickie.

My hoodie tightened around my neck. I was being dragged backward. I kicked and screamed. An arm wrapped around my throat.

"Help!" I shouted.

The streets were filled with the homeless. No one stepped in. No one tried to stop them.

"Where is it?" one of them growled.

"Where's what? Who are you people?" I tried to keep my voice low like Vickie.

"Ha, pretending like you didn't just steal from us. Like I could ever forget your face. It's seared into my brain," Aiden growled into my ear.

"Give it back and we will take it easier on you," another one of The Trips said.

"I...I don't know what you mean. Please, I'm a nobody." I tried to cry, but no tears came out. I was a terrible actor.

Aiden turned me toward him. He stared into my eyes. Licking his lips he pulled me closer. My body reacted to him. Shit. *Get your shit together, Kira. Now is not the time to get wet.* I couldn't stop thinking about him with that woman.

"You are so much more than a nobody." He grabbed a fistful of my hair. "Tell us."

"Fuck you!" I kneed him in the balls.

The other two were on me before I could move my foot. They had me in the air. I tried to kick, but they had my feet. They were strong, shit, they were so strong. I twisted and turned. Nothing.

"Well, she chose the hard way. Now we get to take her home," one of them laughed.

## CHAPTER 4

## *Aiden and the blonde*

ANGER COURSED THROUGH MY VEINS. SHE WAS trouble, I knew it. I knew it from the moment she stepped into my office. I was on the phone, but I couldn't hear a word my grandfather was saying. I only saw her. The defiance was evident from the lack of pigtails. I should have sent her away at that moment.

Instead I showed her exactly where our safe was. How had someone as beautiful and captivating as her become a thief? Ha, it probably helped. I was even fooled.

She kicked at Jason. He held on tight but she had too much fight in her. I sighed and pulled a cloth from my hand. It wasn't my style to chloroform women, but she was too feisty.

"You know that can cause damage to the brain, liver and kidneys?" Jason asked.

I pressed the cloth to her face. "She'll be fine."

She slumped down. Her luscious hair fell in waves down her face. Good, I didn't need to be put into a trance again.

Since she stopped struggling, Derek was able to carry her alone. He cradled her like something precious. Shit, I had seen that look before on him. Not often, but every once in a while he would get a fascination with a girl. He was having it with this one. We couldn't afford for him to catch feelings. Or any of us I reminded myself.

"How did you track her down so easily?" Jason asked. His hands had blood on them. She must have been bleeding from somewhere.

"Pat. He used his connections to find out where you would go if you wanted something stolen. Apparently Kira the finder as she calls herself, is easy to find." I wiped more blood from my nose.

We got in the car and Jason got in the back seat with Derek and the girl. Apparently they both wanted to keep an eye on her. Shit, Jason was looking at her all dewy-eyed.

Yes, she was the most gorgeous woman I had ever seen and her attitude made her even more captivating, but we had to stay focused. My brothers were not going to like what I was going to suggest when we got home.

Derek carried her into the house and Pat came rushing over. Of course he did. That man had a heart of gold. He cared so much about everyone. It was one of the best things about him.

"Boss, is she okay? Did she really steal? She needs medical attention." Pat wiped a tear from his eye.

"No doctor for her. Maybe she will talk if she is in a little bit of pain." I took a handkerchief from my pocket and handed it to him.

He blew his nose and wiped at his face again. Luckily it wasn't the one covered in chloroform.

"Get the cell ready," I demanded.

"Cell?" Jason and Derek asked simultaneously.

We had a cell in our basement. It always seemed barbaric to me. I remembered when I was young my grandfather used to keep people in there. He always said it was for people he

27

would soon put on trial. That was the thing about being Elite, we got to be judge and juror. Those were his words, not mine. I didn't think it was fair, but he did.

In all the times I remembered he held someone for trial, I only remembered one outcome. Death. It was the way things were. Even though we still had an American government most people didn't know that. It was kept secret. That way Elite's could run their countries and America could be defended by a military no one knew existed. It was the perfect balance.

That was unless you consider that Elite's decided who lived and who died. I knew what Jason and Derek were thinking when I suggested putting this woman in the cell. Death. Ha, like I would allow that. No matter how much I hated her for stealing from us, I wouldn't kill her. Well, probably not.

"No," they both said.

"No? Are you two kidding? Listen, she needs to talk and if she won't then she will go on trial." I yanked the woman from Derek's arms before he did something stupid.

"Trial? What are we gonna do? Call in Gramps and his brothers? Then what? They decide to kill her?" Derek went to pull her back into his arms.

"Don't touch her. I see how you look at her. She stole from us! She either talks or she goes on trial. End of discussion." I ground my teeth.

Jason stood there, quiet as always. He never did have much to say, but said everything with his eyes when he didn't talk. He disapproved, maybe even more than Derek. I couldn't figure out why. She stole his work. It was something he developed and yet it looked like he was taking her side.

"You disapprove?" I asked him.

"Yes, No. Look I get it. I know what she stole so let's get on with this." He waved his hand.

I turned and headed toward the basement. Derek, Jason,

and Pat followed. I knew they didn't agree with this, but they would. Maybe when she woke up and tried to break something of theirs they would understand. It took her one lucky shot and she broke my nose. I would have to get it set after this.

Pat grabbed one of the servants on his way down and ordered her to grab some cleaning supplies. He also told her to grab a mattress and blankets which I stopped. She got nothing until she talked to us.

## CHAPTER 5

# *Kira and the cell*

"SWEETIE? SWEETIE, ARE YOU OKAY?" A HAND grazed my face.

I opened my eyes and sat up. Fuck. The bed was metal. Sleeping in the streets didn't prepare me for this bed. It was rusty and harder than the cardboard and blankets I used. Not to mention there were no blankets.

Pat was sitting next to me. He took a wet rag and ran it across my temple. I pushed it aside. "What are you doing?"

"Sweetie, your head. I'm getting the blood off. You must have bumped it." He dipped the rag in a bucket of water.

"Yea, I'm sure it was me and nothing to do with the dick-heads dragging me back here." I touched my forehead. A bump had already swelled. It felt like a cut ran down to my temple.

"They would never hurt a lady." He started to clean me again.

"Stop that, please. They would and they did. Why are you so blinded by them?" I pushed his hand away.

"You don't know them. They are good people." He grabbed my hands. "Trust me, they are."

I looked around the room ignoring him. The guy was obviously brainwashed. The walls were concrete and water dripped down in the corners. A toilet sink combo sat in the corner. Bars made up the fourth wall. I was in a damn cell! Those fuckers locked me up. Here Pat was spewing about them being good people and I was in here.

"Where the hell am I?" I snapped.

"Their basement. They said it's only temporary." Pat stood and backed away. He must have noticed the anger in my face.

"What?" I stood and took a step toward him. I could have easily overpowered him and gotten out of here. The Trips were stupid for leaving me alone with him.

Chains rattled. *You have got to be kidding me!* A single chain was wrapped around my ankle. I jumped toward Pat. I would have to take him down and get the fuck out of here.

Pat backed up against the bars. The chain tightened. I fell forward, on my face. My head was at Pat's feet. They gave me just enough slack to get nowhere. I pulled at the chains. Nothing.

Blood dripped down my face. The fall smashed my nose. It wasn't the first time I had a broken nose, but damn it hurt. I touched my nose, it was crooked. I would have to set it before it started to heal.

"Sweetie, I will be right back. I'll get someone to look at that." Pat shut the gate to my cell behind him and locked it.

Hopefully he would get someone in here that I could get my hands on. If I had a hostage, I could maybe use them as leverage. Maybe.

Two minutes later one of The Trips stood at the gate. He had on jeans and a t-shirt, but I wasn't sure which one it was. Probably not Aiden. He seemed like he would only wear suits. Very businesslike.

"Kira, right?" The Trip unlocked the gate and stepped inside.

There was no way I would be able to take him as a hostage. So I ignored him and put my head between my knees allowing the blood to drip down. I didn't care that it got all over their floor.

"Let me help you." He placed his hand on my back.

I flinched, the pain in my back was worse than my nose. I pinched the brim of my nose, waiting for the blood to clot.

"You have to look at me so I can set it. You don't want it to heal." He placed his hand under my chin.

"Touch me again and you'll need to set your own nose." Oh yea, I had broken Aiden's nose, this definitely wasn't him. So which one was it, the one reading or the one that was fucking?

"I'm only trying to help. You don't have to be so nasty." He dropped his hand.

"She doesn't want help, brother. She would rather bleed all over the floor. Kinda hot, actually." Another of The Trips stepped into the cell.

There wasn't enough space for me there. With them the place seemed to shrink even more. Oh great, the third triplet entered the cell. From the bandage and two black eyes, I knew it was Aiden. Good, served him right.

"Where is it?" Aiden grabbed my wrist and pulled me toward him.

I could smell the rage pouring off of him.

"Tell me now or you will pay!" He pressed his body against mine.

I leaned forward so the blood would drip on his shirt, which was way too close to me. "What are you gonna do? Lock me up? Too late!" I wiggled my ankle so the chain would rattle.

"Trust me, there are way more ways to punish you than just locking you up," he whispered into my ear.

A chill ran down my spine. "Is that supposed to scare me?"

"No it's the truth." He pushed me away from him and I fell onto the metal bed.

"Let's talk this out. No need to get all angry, Aiden." The Triplet that came in second leaned against the wall.

"Derek, you do realize the repercussions of the missing, um, items, right?" the one who tried to fix my nose asked. Which meant he was Jason, the one reading.

"Yea, yea. You all worry too much." Derek waved his hand in the air. "So, Hot Stuff, tell us, you got any family? Cause I'll tell you living with brothers can be a pain sometimes. Ya know?"

"No. No family," I stammered. Vickie was the only person I had. I didn't remember my father and my mother died a few years ago.

Murdered. Not that anyone cared because she was just a homeless person. My stomach turned. She had left to go to work. She cleaned for a living. Rich people never liked cleaning up their own mess.

I waited for hours for her to return. Then days. I went out searching for her. After all, I was Kira the finder, I could find anything. I wished I wasn't so talented. It took a lot of investigating. All clues led to an alley in the outskirts of town. No one went there. It was abandoned.

She was there. Lying on the ground. Her throat was slit. The blood had dried. She had stiffened. I did the best I could to give her a proper burial. Only Vickie and I were at her funeral. I never caught who killed her. It was the only thing I couldn't find.

"So, no one is gonna come looking for you?" Derek

crossed his arms. "That's kinda sad actually. You gotta have friends or something. What do street people do all day?"

"Oh, ya know. Look for ways to mess with The Rich and The Elite. Like stealing from them," I laughed.

"You are such a brat." Aiden ran his fingers through his hair.

"Do you even know what you stole?" Jason lifted my chin again to look at my nose.

"I'm sure whatever it was, you have plenty of. You guys do realize there are millions of homeless people that could use your help." I lifted up my head so Jason could get a better look. I didn't want his help, but I also didn't want a bent nose.

He placed a hand on both sides of my nose. Before I could stop him Aiden got behind me and wrapped his arms around me. His muscles bore into my back and I was pretty sure I felt his cock. Not that I cared.

Jason quickly set my nose. I screamed. Aiden squeezed me tighter. I fought him, twisting and turning. Fuck.

"Shh. You're okay," Aiden whispered.

I turned to look at him because there was no way he just said that. He cut his eyes at me and got up.

"Broken nose or not you are one hot piece." Derek winked at me. "Look, we help plenty of homeless people. We gave you a job and what do you do? Steal from us."

"How does that feel?" Jason asked. He seemed genuinely concerned.

"Like I had my nose reset." I scooted back onto the metal bed. These men were way too close to me. They made thinking hard.

"Look, you have two choices. Give us back what you stole or we will kill you." Aiden shrugged as if neither option mattered to him.

"How about you guys all go fuck yourselves. Or find

another one of those servant girls and you can all fuck her." I crossed my arms.

"Actually little bro doesn't partake in that." Derek pointed to Jason.

"Younger by minutes." Jason turned to me. "No, I don't. Those two do."

"We are getting off track here." Aiden pulled a set of keys from his pocket. "What will it be? We can keep you locked up here for as long as we want." He dangled the keys inches from my face.

That smug asshole. When I got out of there I was going to give him another bloody nose. Shit, I was going to give all of them bloody noses.

"Go fuck yourselves!" I yelled.

Aiden shrugged and left the cell. Jason and Derek followed him and walked from my sight. Aiden locked the door and smiled at me.

## CHAPTER 6

# Kira and the fourth trip

THREE DAYS I STAYED ON THE METAL BED. AT LEAST I thought it was three days. There was no way to actually tell the time. No one came to visit me. The Trips didn't come back to check on me. Not that I cared. I was more concerned about the lack of food and the pain in my back.

It wasn't that I wasn't used to going long stretches without food. But water. They didn't even come in with water. There was a sink attached to the toilet. So I did sorta have water. There was no cup so I had to keep using my hands to get as much as possible. It was more annoying than anything.

My stomach growled, betraying me. When was the last time I had eaten? I couldn't remember. Maybe the morning I stole from them. I couldn't remember what it was. I grabbed my stomach willing it to stop growling. I would not give them the satisfaction of knowing how hungry I was.

Chills ran up my spine. I was so cold. I wrapped my arms around my legs, shaking. It must have been from the lack of food. My back was in so much pain I couldn't even lay on it. I tried but it felt bruised. So when I did sleep it was on my side. I had to get out of here.

I searched the cell for a way out. A loose screw in the floor, a brick in the wall I could pull out. Anything. There was nothing. I tried to get the chain off my ankle. That only resulted in broken and bleeding nails. I wasn't sure how, but I would get out of here.

"Sweetie?" Pat came barreling toward me carrying a tray.

Beef, cheese, and freshly baked bread filled the air. My stomach growled. I needed that food. As he got closer I saw red, green, and orange fruits. Some I didn't recognize. The bread was covered in melted butter. The beef swam in a thick sauce. It was more food than I had ever seen. Was he bringing all that for me?

He set the tray down on the other side of the gate, out of my reach.

"Please, I'm so hungry," I begged.

"I know. I would have come sooner, but they wouldn't let me." He pulled a key from his pocket. "They are awfully mad at you."

"I don't give a shit if they are mad. They deserve to have everything taken from them. Not just one tiny bag." I clenched my fists.

Pat unlocked the gate. "Can't you just tell them whatever they want to know?"

"I can't. I wish you could understand. A part of you has to. You were homeless, right? Or are homeless. Do you live here?" Maybe I could get him to help me.

"My family has worked for the Cartrights since before the new classes were formed. I was born in this mansion. I grew up with The Trips. Please believe me when I say they are good people. The head of the family, well not so much, but don't worry they don't come around here very often." Pat brought in the tray and set it down.

I grabbed it and bit into the bread. It was still warm. I let out a low moan and continued to eat. As I ate, Pat talked.

"You should have seen them when they were younger. Running around the castle playing tricks on everyone. No one could tell them apart. Not even their own mother. Not that she was around much. My mother basically raised them. Oh man. All four of us drove that woman crazy, still do." Pat grabbed a piece of cheese and plopped it into his mouth. "She says that I'm the fourth trip. I agree. We did everything together.

Oh man. I remember when Aiden got his pecker caught in his zipper. You think the broken nose you gave him was bad. Nope, that was worse. Jason has had a nose stuck in a book since before he could read. And Derek, that man. He wanted to be a magician. He read about them when he was little. Thought he could bring the tradition back. His parents put an end to that.

They all have to work in the family business. Real Estate and NanoTechnology. I know they don't actually go together. But that's what they do."

"Why are you telling me all this?" I asked in between bites of beef. It melted in my mouth.

"So you can understand. They are real people. They were raised by a homeless woman, my mother. Yes, we got to live in the mansion instead of on the streets, but that doesn't change our class." He grabbed another piece of cheese. "Whatever you took from them, give it back. Is staying locked up really worth it?"

"I thought they were gonna kill me if I didn't give them what I took?" I asked.

"Like the pot roast? My mom made it. Best cook around." He waved his hands in the air. "Sweetie, I told you they are good people. They would never kill you. Although you are

38

starting to look like death. I'm glad I brought you food when I did."

Well, that made up my mind. There was no way I would ever tell them. Not that I had planned on it anyway. For a brief moment I had considered it. Vickie had to be well on her way to Mexico by now. I could give them the bag and tell Carlos I couldn't complete the mission.

The one thing that was stopping me was Carlos. He had given me 50k as a down payment. What would he do when he found out I had given The Trips back the bag? He wouldn't be okay with it. I didn't know if he was capable of killing. That was something I wasn't okay with. Death wasn't an option for me. One day my life would be better, I just knew it. I would have to stay alive long enough to see that come true.

One day I would get out of here. Maybe sell the bag to Carlos and find my way to Vickie. We would live out our days somewhere on a beach. It would be better than this. Life would be better.

"Pat, I really like you. I think you are a good person. They aren't. No Elite is." I grabbed some cheese and bread from the plate and shoved it in my hoodie for later.

"Hopefully you change your mind soon." Pat grabbed the tray and stood up. "You don't have much time."

"You said they wouldn't kill me."

"It's not them I'm worried about." Pat turned and left.

## CHAPTER 7

# Kira and the guards

I WOKE TO WHISPERS OUTSIDE MY CELL. KEEPING MY eyes shut I strained to hear them. My back bore into the metal. Sharp pains trickled down my legs. I must have rolled in my sleep. Water dripped from the ceiling. A constant drop, drip, drop. I had fallen asleep to that noise, now it was distracting me. Drop, Drip, Drop.

*Concentrate, Kira!*

"We can't keep her," one of them whispered. It sounded like a triplet, maybe Jason.

"We have no choice. She stays," a gruff voice replied. Probably Aiden.

"She isn't some plaything you can keep around," Jason whispered.

"I don't know, that sounds like a lot of fun. Have you seen her?" the man I thought was Derek asked.

"This is not a game. We need to get her to talk," Aiden's voice vibrated as he spoke.

"Gentlemen, she is from the streets. She isn't gonna trust any of you," Pat chimed in.

"So what do you suggest, Pat? Because we have two weeks before the family arrives," Jason said.

"Can we not forget what she stole?" Aidens foot slammed into the ground, or his fist into a wall. I wasn't sure. "If that gets out. If she gave that to anyone, the damage it could do."

"No way it got out. She hid it somewhere. She didn't have time to give it to anyone. Hopefully," Jason said.

"Gotta be hidden. We searched her body. And what a nice body I might add. Did you see those hips? I would love to grab ahold of them and..." Derek practically moaned.

"Enough. We need to get her to talk," Aiden demanded.

"Might I suggest something?" Pat asked. After a few moments of silence he continued. "Befriend her. She thinks you guys are the enemy. Take turns guarding her. Talk to her. Get to know her. You have two weeks before the family arrives and puts her on trial. Take the time to try and get her to trust you. Then she'll talk."

He was out of his mind. I liked Pat, but that was bullshit. *Get to know me? Me, trust them? Never gonna happen.* Not to mention the taking turns guarding me. *What were they gonna do? Sit outside my cell. If they spend all their time with me, I would kill Pat.*

Since the government had failed, The Elites took it upon themselves to hold trials and dole out punishments as they see fit. Most people that were put on trial got minor sentences like clean for a year, for free. It was all ridiculous since half the time they didn't commit any crimes. If it was more serious like murder and anything with a child, they were killed. I didn't even think they had a trial. Just executed right there on the spot.

I saw it happen once. A creepy looking older man with one eye was accused of kidnapping a child. The Elite security guards rolled in and slaughtered him right on the spot. The child was found hours later, he had gotten lost on his way home and had never even heard of the man accused. Nothing happened to the security guards. Now, I wasn't saying people who did awful things shouldn't be punished, but there should be some order to it. And they should have to make sure they had the right person.

So yea, a trial scared the crap outta me. I was guilty of stealing from the wealthiest family for miles, possibly even all the countries in the United States. What would they do to me? That must have been what Pat was talking about when he said he wasn't worried about them. He was worried about their family. Oh man, what were they gonna do to me?

"If you'll excuse me gentlemen. I need to feed our guest," Pat said. That was followed by grunts.

Pat unlocked my cell and sauntered in with a tray filled with eggs and fruit. "I noticed you ate all the strawberries last time, so I brought more."

"Thank you. It's obvious they don't want you feeding me, so why do you?" I sat up and plopped a strawberry in my mouth.

"We do want to feed you, but we also want you to talk!" Derek yelled. After what sounded like a scuffle, footsteps led away from us.

"Yes, at first they thought starving you out would do some good. That was until I explained that homeless people can go a long time without food. They are built from better stuff. Way stronger than any Rich or even Elite." Pat grabbed a strawberry and gossiped like we were old friends.

"How would you know? I know you say you are homeless. But really you aren't. You're practically one of them. And don't think I didn't hear you telling them to get to know me. What kinda crap is that?" I didn't care how much I liked him, he wasn't getting off that easily.

"You know most of the staff here lives on the streets. What? You think I don't talk to them. You think I don't spend

42

all of my free time bringing them food, blankets, clothes. Helping them get jobs." This time his voice was sharp. I had pushed too far.

"I...uh. I didn't know." I shoved eggs in my mouth to stop myself from talking.

"Those men that you hate so much are the reason I am able to do that. They are trying to help. You need to give them back what you stole." Pat stood and left the cell.

"It's not that simple," I muttered.

"Everything in life is that simple. You have a choice and right now Sweetie, you are making the wrong one." Pat locked the gate. "It might do you some good to get to know people outside of your class."

Damn. I sunk down into the metal bunk, no longer hungry. I got that he grew up in this mansion so his values were different. Yet, he spent time with real homeless people and still defended The Trips with everything he had. *Could he be right? No, there was no way he could be.*

He left the food tray. I stared at it. My stomach twisted and turned. I pushed it further away and curled up. I had never been locked up before. Every night I fell asleep in the open air. Not once did I look up and see a roof. It was eerie. I didn't like it. The comfort of walls and a roof should have made this easier. Instead I was claustrophobic.

I wasn't sure how much longer I would be able to handle staying in here. There had to be a way to escape. There had to be.

Two men came into my view carrying a large chair. They both looked beefy and wore that stupid uniform. When they got in front of my cell they dropped it down and turned to me.

"Please, help me." I pulled at the chain and tried to make my voice quiver.

"Geez, they got a girl locked in here." The bigger of the

two turned to me. "Are you okay?"

"No. They...they kidnapped me." I wrapped my arms around my chest. "Please, I don't know what they will do to me."

"Fuck. I can't believe they would lock up some innocent girl." He ran his hand down his face.

"Ha. There is nothing innocent about her, Jamal." One of The Trips slapped him on the back. I would really have to learn which one of them was which.

"Oh. Derek, hi. It's just. Well look at her." Jamal pointed at me.

I batted my eyes and puckered out my bottom lip.

"I see her. She broke Aiden's nose. So unless you want the same thing, I suggest staying away from her. I know she's hard to resist with her hotness and all." Derek flopped in the chair they brought down and pulled the lever for the recliner.

"Damn. Serves her right then. Um. Do you need anything else? Someone else is coming down with food and drinks for you." Jamal cut his eyes at me.

Since the jig was up and he knew I wasn't as innocent as he thought I shrugged and leaned back against the wall. He shook his head and walked away with the other servant. Now, I was left alone with Derek.

The vision of him with a woman sucking on him stayed with me. Every time I looked over at him my cheeks burned. I tried to stay looking at the wall, floor, ceiling, anything but him. A chill ran through me, it seemed like it was constantly there. I wrapped my arms around my knees trying to warm up.

A little while later that same woman came sauntering down with a tray of sandwiches and french fries. She had a stand in her other hand that she propped open next to his recliner. She smiled at him as she set the tray on it. Instead of leaving she picked up a french fry and held it to his lips. Ugh, I wanted to look away, yet I couldn't.

"Thanks Danny, I got this." Derek took the french fry she was trying to feed him. It was the first time his voice didn't have the hint of laughter with it. He appeared cold, disconnected. Just like Aiden.

"You sure? I could feed you something else." Danny winked at him.

"Danny, we talked about this. You deserve better than me. Go find someone that can care about you. That's not me. That's not any of us." Derek looked down as if he was ashamed.

"Oh, I know. I just thought." Danny wiped away a tear.

"I'll talk to Aiden. He can get you a job off-grounds." Derek reached out to grab her arm.

She shrank back. Tears were streaming down her face. She turned and ran away. I heard her cries long after she was gone.

"Did you have to be such a dick?" I tossed a piece of bread at him. It hit the bars and fell.

"This coming from the girl throwing food," he laughed. "We told Pat not to feed you. That man does what he wants."

"So what do you do? Fuck them and then send them off the grounds. I'm surprised you have any workers left." I chucked a strawberry at him. This time it went past the bars, and him.

"Why, you wanna be next?" He raised an eyebrow at me. "But to answer your question. No. We have flings, but they all know it's just that."

"So you and Aiden share every girl? Does Jason ever join?" I pressed my legs together, willing my body to stop getting wet.

Visions of The Triplets on me, around me, caressing me danced in my head. Imagining what it would be like to have one of them inside me while the other kissed me. The third massaging my chest. I had never been with any man, yet alone three. *Would it be better? Could I handle it?*

"You just got all squirmy there. You thinking about it?" Derek grinned then took a sip of his drink.

He got up and walked over to the bars. His gray sweatpants showed off his extremely large package. *Stop, don't look there.* He reached through the bars to hand me the drink. I scooted back. I would rather drink from the sink than take anything from him.

"It's wine. Might help take the edge off." He shrugged when I didn't move and went back to his recliner.

He sat back in his chair, put his hands behind his head and stared at the ceiling. For hours I watched him, refusing to speak again. I didn't want to hear anymore about his sex capades. Well really, I didn't want to have any more visions. I had to keep reminding myself he held me captive. He was an asshole. A wretched, horrible man with a sexy jawbone and hands that begged to be all over me.

No. I would not think like that. Ugh, why did my captors have to be so hot? I clenched my fists. This was not the way to think. I had to focus on getting out of here. There had to be something I could do. I needed a plan and one that didn't involve ending up in bed with The Trips.

Pat came and went. He brought food for both of us. He had tried to talk to me but I wasn't in the mood. Lack of open air and sun was starting to get to me. Not to mention the only thing I could do was stare at Derek. Not that it was a terrible view but it put ideas in my head that I didn't need.

My stomach clenched. Oh no. I had to go to the bathroom. I looked over at the metal toilet. It was in full view of Derek. If it was just a tinkle maybe I could have. It wasn't, of course it wasn't. There was no way. I had to hold it. *He can't watch me all day, right?*

Twenty minutes later and my stomach was in full blown panic mode. If I didn't go soon it was going to be a whole lot worse. Maybe he would give me some privacy. It was the least he could do.

"Um, Derek." I tried to use my sweet imitation of Vickie's voice.

He turned his wrist to look at his watch. "Sorry, Hot Stuff. Whatever you gotta say will have to wait until my next shift." He got up and walked away.

*Yes, I'm alone!* I rushed over to the toilet and pulled down my pants just as Aiden approached. It had to be him because of the blue suit and crisp white shirt. He stood at the bars and stared at me. My hoodie wasn't long enough to stretch past my waist. So I was literally standing there with my pants around my ankles, exposed. *Did he just lick his lips?*

"Please, give me some privacy," I begged, covering my bits.

"I do like when you beg." He placed a hand on the bars.

"Please, I'm serious." My stomach clenched, again.

"Okay. I'll be back in a few minutes. Then we get to spend the next few hours together. Do you need anything? A change of clothes. Hot bath. The key to the cell." He half grinned then turned and left.

"Asshole," I muttered.

## CHAPTER 8

## Kira and the bathtub

AS PROMISED HE WAS BACK A FEW MINUTES LATER. Luckily it didn't take me too long to handle my business and I was back on the metal bunk when he came back. I avoided looking at him when he approached the bars again.

Aiden took out a key from his pocket and unlocked the gate. Oh, great. He was gonna threaten my life again. The joys. Or maybe he was gonna kill me and be done with it. Either way I wasn't telling him where the bag was.

He stepped inside the cell and motioned for me to stand. So like a good girl, I sat there with my arms crossed. He snapped his fingers. Ha, that wasn't going to work. Ever.

"Stand," he demanded.

"Fuck off," I demanded.

He grabbed my arm and pulled me to my feet. My back was on fire, my body ached. I was so cold. I could have tried to fight him. The gate was open. How far could I get? I wasn't even sure where in the house I was. There was no way I would get far. No, my escape would have to be when they didn't know I was leaving.

Aiden turned me to face the wall. If he tried anything with

me, I would kill him. Nothing against Vickie, but I didn't hook. As hot as this guy was, that didn't mean he could take advantage of me.

He pressed his face into my hair and sniffed. "You stink."

"Gee, I wonder why. I'm sure it has nothing to do with being locked up." I elbowed him. He grabbed my arm before it made contact.

The cuffs clicked down on my wrists before I realized what he was doing. That bastard handcuffed my hands behind my back. Whatever kind of kink he was into, it wasn't happening. Ugh, could I stop thinking of him naked for two seconds?

"Lift your foot, so I can unlock the shackle," he growled into my ear.

"Why?" I asked.

His body was so close to mine. I could feel him pressed against me. I wanted more than anything to be turned around and stripped naked. For some reason having him, or really any of them close turned my brain to mush. I could smell the citrus of his cologne. His scruff would feel amazing against my skin.

Instead of responding he bent down and pulled my foot up to him. The click of the chain around my ankle felt freeing. Yea I was still handcuffed but the weight was gone. I wanted to turn and run. To get to Mexico and find Vickie.

He pulled at me to go with him. I had no idea why but he was leading me out of the cell. Shit, maybe he was going to kill me. Or maybe his family showed up early and they would kill me.

The stairs were rickety and creaked as he dragged me up them. For so much money he sure did have a run down part of the house. It didn't take long before we were out of the crappy part and back into the immaculate mansion.

I stumbled more times than I could count as I walked. Little stars clouded my vision. I tried to stay focused. For some reason my body was failing me. Probably from having me in a cold cell for days.

Not a single servant stopped what they were doing. In fact, most averted their eyes as if they didn't see me. Was it normal for Aiden to be walking a handcuffed woman covered in dry dirt and blood? I hadn't seen a mirror but I was sure I had two black eyes.

Now that I was up and moving around I could feel the pain in my back. Vickie hadn't had time to fully bandage me up from falling in the bushes. *Had it gotten infected? Probably not.*

Either way it stung. Little sharp razors strung across my back. I was sure it didn't help sleeping on a metal bunk. I kept making excuses, but the reality was, I was pretty sure I was getting sick.

Aiden stopped in front of the door with two deadbolts.

"Oh, hell no!" I yelled. "Help! Please!"

"Would you relax?" He shoved me inside.

"I will not relax. You think I'm gonna fuck you." I stumbled forward and almost fell before he caught me. "Maybe have your brother join. I would rather die."

"Maybe someday you will beg me to fuck you. Most women do," he whispered in my ear.

Inside the room was the sofa where Derek and Aiden tag teamed Danny. There was a large bed set across from a fireplace. In the middle of the room was a tub. It was bigger than the dumpster I slept beside.

Lavender and vanilla filled the room. Steam rose from the tub. Bubbles floated on the top. Two women dressed in the Cartright uniform with pigtails stood by it. One waved her hand as if presenting it to me.

"What kind of kinky crap are you into?" I turned to Aiden. "Not that I'm knocking your yum, it's just not my thing."

"You stink like an infection." He unlocked my handcuffs. "My security is right outside the door so don't try anything. These girls will help you."

"Help me what?" I asked.

"Bathe. Derek noticed blood on the back of your hoodie and what might be puss. They will help clean you. Then get on the bed faced down. A doc is gonna come check out your wounds." He went and sat on the sofa, facing away from me. "Don't worry I won't look."

I had never taken a bath. Shit, I was lucky to take showers when I got the chance. I wanted to take off running. I wanted to leave. Instead I kicked off my sneakers.

The women came over and helped me out of my clothes. I would have done it myself had I been able to get the hoodie off. It was stuck to my back. Maybe it was infected. My body ached.

They helped me into the tub. The warm water engulfed me. I moaned as I fully sunk in. My back stung. My legs were stiff from being in the cell on that damn bed. I hadn't realized how much pain I was in until I stepped into the water.

"Lean forward so I can get your back," the older woman with gray hair and a wicked smile said.

"Oh, no It's okay," I stammered. Never had someone washed me. My mind grew fuzzy.

"Would you stop being so damn stubborn!" Aiden yelled from the sofa.

I did as I was told and leaned forward. The younger woman with mousy features and a grim look gasped, "That looks really bad."

Aiden was there before I realized he got up. His hand was on my shoulder pushing me forward slightly. A low rumble escaped his throat.

I covered my breast with my arms and hoped the bubbles covered the rest. "Look I'm sure it's not that bad."

"Fuck. The doc needs to see you now. There are thorns embedded in your back. Your entire back is bruised. " He let out a low groan. "Why didn't you say anything?"

"When would I have? When you locked me in the cell? When you kidnapped me? Oh wait, I know, when you had me sleep on a damn metal bunk for days!" I snapped.

The younger woman rushed out of the room. The concern in his voice had me worried. If someone that hated me and threatened to kill me was worried then I should have been too. Of course had they not kidnapped me, Vickie would have fixed this and it never would have gotten infected.

Aiden reached into the tub. The arms of his suit got soaked as he put his arms under me. I wanted to protest. Wanted to tell him not to touch me. Instead for a brief moment I welcomed the comfort his arms provided.

The corners of my vision were turning black. Shit maybe it was bad.

He brought me over to the bed and set me down. With his help I rolled over onto my stomach. I tried not to think of him looking at me naked. Something soft and fluffy rolled across my skin. He was drying me off with a towel.

I looked up at him to thank him. His suit jacket and shirt had been removed. Nevermind. I had to look away. He was just too sexy. And with me being naked, it wasn't a good combination. I felt as though I was fading and yet I was thinking about him. What was wrong with me?

Once he was done he draped a sheet over me. I was so cold a shiver ran through me, I wanted the heat from the tub again. The air in the room was heavy. The lights were too bright. How did I not notice that before?

People rushed into the room. Derek, Jason and a woman that must be the doc came right over to the bed. Before I could do or say anything, the sheet was pulled back.

"What did we do to her?" Jason asked. "This isn't right."

"I say that's on her. Had she not stolen from us none of this would have happened." Derek pointed at me. "But this is bad. Doc, is she gonna die? No one that pretty should die. Not like this."

"Would you guys stop bickering?" She opened her bag and pulled out a needle. "She is burning up. This isn't good."

"What's that for? I asked.

"Antibiotics. It's to stop the infection. I'm also gonna have to numb your back. Those thorns need to be removed and the wounds cleaned. It looks like at least one of them is gonna need stitches, maybe two." She jabbed the needle in my arm. "You may have gone septic. I don't know how you are still functioning at this point."

I like the way she talked to me. She didn't talk down to me like I was a homeless person. She made me feel like an equal, or maybe the infection was messing with my head.

She pressed a thermometer to my head. When she pulled it away she tsk'd. "How long has she been like this? This looks like days!" She snapped at the men.

They all looked to the ground, ashamed.

"Maybe a couple days." Aiden raked his hand across his face. "Is she gonna be okay?"

"I don't know." The Doc jabbed another needle into my arm.

The world grew fuzzy. It was as if someone put a sheet over everything. I tried to move. My eyes drooped. Nothing was working. The Doc faded in and out.

"The infection is bad," The Doc whispered.

My mother was there. She drifted over to me as if she was an angel. Her long blonde hair cascaded down her shoulders. I reached out to her. She grabbed my hand and kissed it. *I'm here.*

I blinked and she was gone. Aiden was holding my hand. Derek was caressing my hair. Jason cupped my face. They were all there by the bedside. Worry spread across their faces. It was as if they cared. I must have been in worse shape than I thought.

"I'm here," Aiden whispered. His lips grazed my hand.

It was the last thing I heard before I went to sleep.

## CHAPTER 9

## Aiden and the brothers

I GRABBED THE TENNIS BALL FROM MY DESK. Tossing it from hand to hand didn't do shit for my stress. I wanted to scream, punch something, hurt someone, fuck someone. Anything to stop myself from thinking of that nuisance that walked into my life.

"Fuck!" I chucked the tennis ball at the wall.

The door swung open.

"Woah." Derek ducked down, avoiding the ball.

"Ouch." Jason rubbed his chest. He hadn't been so lucky.

"Any word?" I asked. They knew what I was referring to. It had been thirty minutes and nothing yet. The doc sent us away, blaming us. That was not our fault. She should have said something.

"No, Pat said he would let us know." Jason slumped into a chair. "What did we do?"

"She stole from us!" I slammed my hands on the desk. "Did you forget that? It's her fault she is on the verge of.... You know."

"Dude, chill. She'll be fine." Derek plastered a fake smile across his face. "That chick is tough. Stop worrying you two."

I sat down trying to ignore the lie in his voice. Both of my brothers were worried. Not that it should have mattered if the thief died. It shouldn't have. She was a low class, nothing, that came into my life just to ruin it.

The day she walked into my office I should have known something was different about her. The way she walked and carried herself wasn't normal. All of my servants had a certain self-doubt within them. It showed in everything they did. But not her. She was full of confidence, right down to her refusal to put her hair in pigtails. Man, I should have fired her.

My cell phone buzzed in my pocket. Ugh. I didn't have time for anyone's shit right now. I pulled it out to hit the ignore. It was my Grandfather. *Fuck*. That was one call I couldn't ignore.

I answered it and put it on speaker.

"Hey Grandfather, we are all here," I answered.

"Good. I trust you three have managed to get the party preparations ready. Myself and the lawyer will be there a day early to finalize everything," he rushed, already sounding ready to be off the phone.

"You can trust us, Gramps," Derek grinned. "Even Jason is in the partying mood."

"I doubt that. No matter. Are there any problems we need to discuss?"

I looked up at the Van Gough painting. How could I tell him the Nant-bots were missing? Of all the things she could have stolen from us. If I told Grandfather, he would insist on coming early. He would torture Kira.

If we couldn't find out where she put the Nant-bots he would have to get involved. The trial would start when the family was all here. None of them would allow her to live.

"Are Mom and Dad coming?" Jason asked.

"No. They have business in Japan." Grandfather sighed. I wondered if he was missing them as well. It had been years since any of us had seen them. They took off for what they called business and never returned. Since Grandfather and myself were the two people who handled most of the business, we knew that was a load of shit.

"Yea, sightseeing and pretending like they don't have family," Derek snapped. He was always so carefree, unless it came to our parents.

"Enough. That'll be all Grandfather. Tell Grandma we love her and can't wait to see her in a few weeks. We have everything under control." I ran my fingers through my hair while staring at the picture.

"Good, cause if anything goes wrong I won't be able to sign over the entire business to you kids. I want to retire, so don't let me down." Grandfather clicked off the phone without saying goodbye.

I slammed the phone down on the desk. If he found out about the Nant-bots that would be it. He would not only kill Kira, he wouldn't retire. Everything was dependent on that Brat telling us what she did with them.

"Well if she dies I guess we don't have to worry about the fam putting her on trial," Derek said. He always could read my thoughts.

"The Nant-bots are useless without the codes." Jason sat forward placing his hands on his knees.

"Look, we have two major problems and both are tied to that damn girl! One of you go and see if she is alive. I'll be back." I ground my teeth and stormed out of the office. *I didn't have time for this. That girl was going to cause me so many damn problems.* I had to get away. I had to think of something else, anything else.

The house wasn't big enough to get away from my brothers or Kira. I could have left, but that wouldn't have solved anything. I had to be here when she got better and started talking. I just wanted to grab her by the hair and force her to tell me where the Nant-bots were. Shaking my head I tried to get that vision out of my head.

There was so much more I wanted to do to her. I wanted to grab her alright. I also wanted to kiss every inch of her. Lick between her legs. Feel what it's like to be inside her. Shit. I couldn't think like that.

I couldn't think of her spread across my knees while I spanked her. Soft and tender at first. Building up until she begged for more. Until she wanted me to spank her ass so hard it left a red mark across her bare skin. Then I would watch as Derek kissed the tender skin. I would wait until she was ready again.

Then I would spank even harder. Purposefully I would graze my fingers across her pussy. She would be wet, and waiting. Then I would allow Derek to run his tongue across her slit. I could hear her beg for more. Maybe I could even convince Jason to join in. He never had, but maybe for her he would. The joy we could give her.

Fuck. My dick was pressed against my pants begging to be released. If I didn't nut soon, someone was gonna be hurting.

I entered my bedroom and slammed the door. Things rattled. A book fell from the shelf. I didn't care. Unzipping my pants I released my dick. Finally, it was in my hands. I kept thinking of spanking her as I stroked myself. Quick jerks except at the tip. I slowly rolled over the tip to increase the pleasure.

Knock. Knock.

*Seriously?*

I pulled harder, faster. I needed to nut.

Knock. Knock.

I put him back and answered the door. It could have been news of her. Then after she told us where our stuff was, I would make my visions a reality.

It was Jane. She flicked her eyelashes at me. There was no

way she knew anything of Kira, she wouldn't even have the clearance to know who the girl was or what we wanted with her. Jane pulled on the bottom of her shirt.

Ugh. I knew what she wanted and any other time I wouldn't deny her. She was cute, had nice curves and wicked thick lips. I had thought about them around my cock before. But tonight I couldn't stop thinking of that bitch, Kira.

"You seemed stressed when you came in here, Sir. I was hoping I could help." Jane twirled her pigtail between her fingers.

Any other time, I would have loved this. Any other time! I pinched the bridge of my nose. Was I really about to turn down those lips? No, I could do her. It would relieve the pressure in my nuts.

"Not right now." My dick had gone soft from the aggravation. I slammed the door.

"Well, whenever you want it, I'm here!" she yelled from the other side of the door.

I paced the room attempting to think of anything else. There were so many things I could have been doing to occupy my time. Number one was to run my business. There were plenty of real estate decisions that needed to be made. There were also a ton of tech decisions in the lab awaiting my approval. None of them mattered right now. I laughed. None of them had mattered since that brat walked into my office.

I had to get her out of my mind. Once she was healed, I would find a way to get her to talk. Maybe if I told her the truth of what she stole. Then she would understand why we needed them back. Would she even care? Jason was right, without the coding they wouldn't work. But if she knew how to code. Did she know what she stole? Maybe she did. Either someone paid her to take them or she did it on her own. If she did it on her own it would have been to destroy them. Why else would she want them? If someone paid her and they had them, we were all fucked.

I squeezed my forehead, this was getting me nowhere. I had no clue why she stole my Nant-bots. I had no clue how to get her to talk. Shit, I didn't even know if she was gonna live. Being out of control like this was wreaking havoc on me. I didn't like it one bit.

Knock. Knock.

"Come in," I shouted. Hopefully it wasn't someone else trying to have sex with me.

Pat stepped into the room and clasped his hand in front of him. He was my head servant. The man kept everyone else in line. If it wasn't for him I would be lost. I told him as much once and he blushed so hard, I decided to never tell him again. He was also the only one with enough guts to tell me how it is.

"Yes, Pat." I waved him inside.

"Sir, I understand Kira did something very terrible. I am not one to deny that. In fact I am one of the few that knows what she stole, so I get it. I'm not defending her. I know she did wrong," Pat rambled.

"Please get to the point, Pat." I got up and walked over to the mini bar I had. I poured myself a whiskey.

"You have her locked in a cell," Pat snapped.

I poured him a whiskey and handed it to him. He took a small sip and smacked his lips.

"Yes, I know. It's where a thief belongs." I waved my glass around.

"She is a good person." Pat stomped his foot. That was one of the things I loved about the man. He stood up against me, even though he knew at any moment I could snap and fire him. I wouldn't, but he didn't know that.

"She is a thief. We caught her. Remember?" I took a gulp of whiskey. How could he forget that?

"I know. But I know people. And I know she had a good

reason. Just because we don't know it, doesn't mean it isn't good." Pat placed his glass down. "I'm going to fix up her cell. You may insist she needs to be in there, but I insist it needs to be fit for a human!"

"Fine. She gets a mattress and a blanket." I pointed my finger at Pat. "That's it!"

"You almost killed her and you think a mattress is enough? Sir! What has gotten into you? This is not you." Pat crossed his arms.

"I have to get her to talk. You think she is gonna want to talk if she is sleeping on silk sheets and cotton pillows or whatever fluffy things you want to put in her room!" I poured another glass.

"Yes, I do. Be nice to her and she just might open up to you." Pat walked over and grabbed my hand. "Sir, you are a good kind man. Deep under the exterior. Sometimes you need reminding of that. I will not allow you to keep treating this girl like this. I will prepare her room. And then when she is better, talk to her. Tell her what the Nant-bots are. Maybe she will tell you where they are."

The door flew open. There were only two people that would open my door without knocking. Both of them were standing there. Jason and Derek stood in the doorway heaving for air. They must have ran to my room.

Shit. That either meant she was awake or dead.

"Doc wants to see us," Derek panted.

## CHAPTER 10

## *Kira and the walk*

THE LIGHTS WERE TOO BRIGHT. THE BED WAS TOO soft. I rolled over. Fuzz or fluff, something got caught up in my mouth. I pulled away. Spitting out the fuzz, I tried to focus on what was right in front of me. It was pink.

Blinking a few more times I tried again to make out what it was. It was too big, too soft, too unnatural. I didn't even know where I was. I couldn't think of that, all I could concentrate on was what the heck I was looking at.

"What did the turtle say to the sloth?" a voice called from the distance.

"Huh?" I mumbled unsure what they were saying or why they were saying it to me. Who was talking?

"Let's take it slooooooow," the voice laughed. "Get it. Cause they are both slow."

Something squeezed my left leg. It tightened around it, like a massage. Not too tight, just an odd sensation. Once that one was done the other one started. I ripped the blanket from me. Two white contraptions were wrapped around my legs. They took turns squeezing my legs.

"It's to keep your blood flow, I think," one of The Trips said.

I looked around. There was an IV in my hand. On the side of the bed was a bag filled with pee. Which meant I probably had a catheter in me. What had they done to me? It was all coming back to me. The Triplets, the bag I stole, the bushes, the pain in my back, the cell.

My mother was there. Wait, no. I imagined that. I imagined The Trips too. They had caressed me, told me they were there for me. It was in my head. None of that was real.

Now I was back in my cell, but it was different. There was a mattress, blankets, pillows, and what I realized was a pink stuffed sloth. Someone took the time to make my cell...comfy. It didn't seem like something The Trips would be concerned with. If I had to guess, I would have assumed it was Pat. All the pinks and grays that decorated my cell seemed like something he would do.

"Who did this to me?" I lifted my hand to show him my IV.

"The Doc. She will be by later to check on you," The Trip replied. He had a hint of laughter to his voice. Which meant it was probably Derek.

"Why? You guys don't seem like the type to give a fuck about someone like me." I shoved my hand in the contraption around my leg. It was hot and itchy. This thing was going to have to come off.

"You mean a hot, sexy little thing? Yea totally not our type. Ha." Derek lifted his head back and fake laughed at me.

"Is everything about sex with you?" I found the velcro and tore off the contraption around my leg.

"Yea. Isn't it with you?" He stood and walked over to the gate. "You shouldn't take those off. Doc is not gonna be happy."

"No." I was leaving out the part that I had never actually

had sex. I mean I had fooled around with a few guys, but that was it. "These things are hot around my legs. I can't take it anymore."

"It should be. Sex is life, literally. You know you could wrap those hot legs around me." Derek licked his lips.

For a moment I contemplated it. What it would feel like to have his strong, hard body between my legs. He had to be experienced. He had so many flings, that there was no way he was awful in bed. Vickie had told me that some men had no clue how to please a woman. All they cared about was getting theirs and then they were done. She called them one pump chumps. There was no way Derek was one of those people.

I was certain all three of The Trips knew how to please women. Even Jason who seemed to have no interest in his brother's way of banging women and then disposing of them. I had bet Jason dated women for long periods of time. Maybe that was why he didn't share. He knew how Aiden and Derek were.

My legs were achy. I needed to move them. How long had it been since I stood on them? I sat up and scooted to the end of the bed. Even though I had a catheter in and an IV I was going to stand. My legs were getting restless.

Before I had the chance to push off from the bed Derek was there. When had he opened the gate? Had it been open the whole time? I guessed they weren't concerned with me running away. Not that I could get very far.

"What are you doing?" Derek asked. His voice was filled with concern. Probably because he wanted my legs around him.

"Getting up. I can't stay like this." I waved my hand around.

"Fine." Derek scratched his head. "If you must, give me a few minutes. I'll get the doctor in here. If she gives you clearance, I'll walk you around."

"Or, I get up now and you can't do shit to stop me." I pointed to the gate. "I'm already locked up. What more can you do?"

"Look, if she gives you clearance, I'll take you for a walk outside." Derek cupped my face.

His hand against me sent a chill through my body. I leaned into his touch. *Shit. Kira, concentrate.* "And what if she doesn't?"

"Then you lay your ass back down and obey her instructions." Derek pulled his hand away.

"You seem serious, you are Derek, right?" I had assumed it was him without asking.

"Duh, you couldn't tell. I'm the sexiest triplet." Derek grinned.

For a moment, my heart melted. I laughed. There was no sexiest triplet. They were impossible to tell apart. Yet, Derek was making jokes and I was laughing. Ugh. I had to stop this. I had to keep reminding myself, they were keeping me prisoner. They were the bad guys.

"Deal?" Derek asked when I still hadn't said anything about listening to The Doc.

Getting outside could prove useful. If I could learn where I was in correlation to getting out of the mansion, that would be useful. Once I had the chance I could escape. Then I could meet Vickie in Mexico. "Deal," I replied.

It didn't take long for The Doc to arrive. She wasn't too pleased with me removing the 'socks' that were around my legs. That was what she called them. I said they were death traps.

After a little bit of back and forth she agreed to remove the IV and catheter. I had to promise to drink lots of water and rest as much as possible. Since I was trapped in a cell I didn't think the resting part would be too hard. It was a bit odd that she didn't mention anything about me being in a cell. Like that part didn't matter to her.

It must have been because I was homeless. Yes she was a doctor but that only took kindness so far. Only the Rich could afford that type of education. They became doctors to help themselves and The Elite. They didn't roam the streets looking for new patients to help.

"So, she can take a stroll?" Derek asked the doc.

"Yes, but be mindful and have a wheelchair ready in case." She pointed at me. "Don't push yourself too far."

I nodded but was already looking around for my pants to put on. There was a new shelf in the room. It had a cup, some toiletries, and a vase on the top shelf. Underneath that was some clothing folded up. I went through them. A pair of sweatpants, t-shirt, underwear, and three skirts. I shook my head, I had a strong feeling the skirts were Derek's idea.

Once the doc was gone, I started getting dressed. It proved harder than I thought. My legs were weak, my back still in pain. The infection must have been worse than I thought.

Stumbling, I grabbed onto the closest thing to me. It was Derek. He scooped me up and placed me on the bed. I went to grab my pants and he took them from my hand.

"Stop being so stubborn. I know we made a deal for a walk but maybe you should rest. Or wear one of the skirts." He grinned.

"Funny. I just lost my balance. I got this." I reached for the pants again.

He swatted my hand away. Reluctantly I lifted my leg for him to dress me. He was gentle. Even though my bits were exposed he seemed to not look. He quickly slid on my pants, he even lifted my bottom to slide them over. He didn't make one comment or make a quick graze over anything. It was like he respected me.

"Huh," I let out a sigh of shock.

"What?" he asked as he grabbed my hoodie to put on me.

"For someone with sex always on the mind, you are being very respectful." I lifted my arms so he could put my hoodie on me.

"I would love nothing more than to fuck you senseless. Maybe one day you will ask me to. Until then, I'll be a perfect gentleman." He stood and helped me to my feet.

Heat rose to my cheeks. He so easily talked about fucking. I looked down so he couldn't see my embarrassment. Images of him receiving a blow job from that woman flooded my mind. Would that be how it would be, or would he take care of my needs? Or would we take care of each others? I shook my head, it didn't matter. It would never happen.

"Thinking about it?" He took my hand in his and walked me out of the cell. "All you have to do is ask. But I do warn you, one time may not be enough. I fear it would be more than a fling."

I opened my mouth and all that came out was a weird strangled sound. He did not say that. *More than a fling? What did that mean?* Nope, it didn't matter. The second I could, I was gone. Then this sexual attraction, or whatever it was would be gone. Soon, none of this would matter, I just needed a way out.

"Where are you two going?" Another of the trips entered the basement. From the suit and anger, I assumed it was Aiden.

"A walk. Doc said it was okay." Derek guided me to the stairs.

"Are you kidding? Do you want her to escape again?" Aiden grabbed my arm, yanking me into him. I lost my balance and slumped into his chest. "Or worse, get hurt again."

Derek scooped me into his arms. I could walk, I didn't need him holding me. Damn, he smelled good. Nope, I wiggled trying to get down. "I can walk."

He set me down. "She can barely walk. I'll make sure nothing happens to her."

"Fine. Anything happens to her and it's on you." Aiden turned back up the stairs.

By the time we got to the top of the stairs Aiden was gone. I didn't know or care where he went. Nor was I thinking about his quip about me getting hurt. In his mind how would that be worse than me escaping. Nope, I didn't care.

I had to concentrate on where we were going. Once I had the chance I would be gone. I would grab the bag and sell it to Carlos. Then, Vicki and I would be reunited. I knew she had made it to Mexico. She was on a beach right now, drinking cocktails and enjoying her freedom.

The exit was right at the top of the stairs. It wasn't even locked. He opened the door while keeping his other arm around me. I was slow going, but he didn't seem to mind. In fact he appeared like the type of man to take his time with everything. I didn't feel like I was slowing him down.

Their backyard was a masterpiece. Bushes carved into sculptures lined the yard. Each one represented a zodiac sign. A brick fountain flowed in the center. Rose bushes and vines trickled up short walls that were placed all around. Benches were placed inside mini gardens. A hot tub the size of a grocery store was in the corner, along with a pool the length of their house. My mouth fell open. People really lived like this while others slept beside dumpsters.

"Like it?" Derek guided me toward the closest bench.

"Yea, it's beautiful and sad." I remained standing so I could stretch out my legs.

"Why is it sad?" He scrunched up his face.

"You guys live like this while others suffer." I searched for an exit. Their backyard was fenced in. On the far end, near the pool there was a gate. That would be how I got out of here.

"So would it be better if we lived on the streets as well?"

His eyes widened. He was shocked I had insulted his way of life.

"No, but do you need all of this? No ya don't." I practically stomped my feet. A few of the servants were in the gardens weeding and cleaning.

"Agreed, but I will enjoy what I have. And no one will make me feel bad about that. Life is meant to be enjoyed." He stood and grabbed my hands. "You could have all of this with me. Just give us what you stole and you can stay. You and I can be something. I know you feel it." He brought my hands to his lips.

That was what this was all about. He wanted the bag. He didn't want me. Someone like him could never want someone like me. Not that I had considered his offer. Well maybe for a split second. If I was someone else I could consider being with him. Shit, I had been thinking of being with all three of The Trips since I walked into their mansion.

A tug pulled at my pant leg. I looked down. A tiny puppy was chewing on my pants. I bent and scratched behind his ear. In response he licked me right across the face. I was in love. This little doggie was the cutest I had ever seen.

"I could give you the world," Derek whispered in my ear.

I looked up to see a woman running with a collar in her hand. She must have been the one in charge of the puppy, or his owner. She wore the bumble bee uniform with pigtails so there was no way she owned this cute little guy.

As she got closer a familiarity swam over me. Maybe it was the pain medication. Or the fact that I had been laying in bed with an infection. It could have been because I was thinking about her. Whatever it was, it was odd that the woman had the same long braids and beautiful smile as Vickie. If I didn't know she was in Mexico, I would have thought it was her.

"Hey Kira, I was hoping they would let you out soon. I

have missed you." The woman who looked exactly like Vickie wrapped her arms around me.

"Who are you?" I blinked. There was no way Vickie was here.

"Are you okay?" She pulled away from me. "It's me, Vickie."

## CHAPTER 11

# *Kira and the dream*

I PUSHED HER AWAY. THERE WAS NO WAY SHE WAS here. There was no way she would have stayed after everything I gave up for her. *Why would she do that?* I wanted to strangle her. Hit her. Do something.

"Sit down." She tried to escort me to the bench.

"I don't need help. What are you doing here?" I slapped her hand away. "I told you to go."

"Kira, you are my only family. You are it. I have no one else." She picked up the puppy and started stroking his short cream fur.

"What does that have to do with why you are here?" I snapped. This was all wrong. She shouldn't be here.

"Did you really think I was going to leave you? Never." She sat on the bench. "After these knuckleheads took you I waited for you. I thought you would have escaped. I waited and waited. Then they found me and offered me a job. I won't leave without you."

Yea, she could be stubborn, but I thought she would listen. I thought she would have left. I would have caught up with her when I had the chance. Now that she was here everything was ruined. I would have to break us both out when the time came.

Since most of her skin was exposed in the skimpy uniform, I inspected it. It was the first time since she started hooking that she didn't have a single bruise. Even the customers that she claimed were gentle, weren't. They all left marks. A smile played in the corner of her lips.

She was happy. Like, really happy. It was a tiny miracle in itself. Being employed by The Trips meant she didn't have to sell herself to strangers. It made me thankful for them. It wasn't Mexico, but until I could get us there, she was safe.

Vickie set down the puppy and pulled me out of earshot from Derek. Until this point he was just observing and listening to everything.

"Look, I know you think Mexico is our freedom, but this life isn't so bad. They told me if you just give back what you stole then you are free to go or stay. They would employ us both. Could you imagine? Legit jobs for both of us." Vickie stared into my eyes, pleading with me.

*Was she right? Was this so terrible?* People would do anything for a job like this. We could even try and work our way up to stay on the property. Our lives would be different, better even. It was my birthday wish coming true.

I shook my head. It wasn't enough for me. Vickie and I deserved total freedom. Not a life where we would always be homeless. No. We needed to get out of here. We needed to go to a place where The Elite and The Rich didn't rule every-thing. Mexico had a government and housing for all. We had to go. The only way to afford it was to sell that bag to Carlos.

"No, I'm sorry, but I will get us out. We deserve the best life. In Mexico we would just be people. Not homeless." I pulled Vicki into me. "Trust me, I'll get us both out.

"Time to go," Derek said. *Did he hear us?*

I turned to scan his face. Nothing had changed. He still

wore that happy smirk. If he had heard, he wasn't acting like he did.

"Can't I stay a little longer?" I batted my eyes at him.

"My shift was over an hour ago. I have something I need to get to." He wrapped his arm around me. "We can come back out here tomorrow. I'll make sure Vickie is here."

"I love you," Vickie called out as we walked away.

My heart crumpled as I entered my cell. Vickie was here. No matter how many times I went over it in my head, I didn't believe it. Everything I had done so far was with the knowledge that she was far from here. I was so wrong. Now, I would do whatever I had to, to get us both out. Even if I had considered giving The Trips the bag, there was no way I could now.

I fell asleep to thoughts of breaking out of here and grabbing Vickie on the way out. Of course, my dreams were the complete opposite.


*Jason entered my cell first. He was naked, erect, and his eyes were filled with lust. He slipped behind me and sat me up. I didn't realize I was also naked until his hands were on my shoulders. Oil slid between his fingers as he massaged me.*

*I moaned as he released the tension I was holding. His hands slowly moved forward. He rubbed my chest avoiding my nipples. I pushed forward wanting his touch. Needing him to caress my nipples. His hand ran down between my breasts massaging, caressing, taunting.*

*Derek entered second. He was also naked and incredibly ready. A smile played at his lips. When our eyes met he grinned. He knew how wet I was becoming. Instead of saying anything he sat on the edge of the bed. Grabbing my foot he started massaging it. I moaned louder as he rubbed oil on me. Then up my calves. I needed him to rub my pussy. His hands never strayed past my knees.*

*My pussy throbbed. Jason caressed my chest still avoiding my nipples. Derek rubbed my legs refusing to get close to what I really wanted.*

"Please," I begged.

"Please, what?" Aiden asked entering the cell. Of course he was in his black slacks and no shirt.

"I...I..." Each time I tried to speak I couldn't form words.

"What do you want, Kira?" Aiden asked. He lifted my chin to look him in the eyes.

*His brothers continued to rub me. Neither said a word. Neither stopped teasing me. My pussy continued to throb, begging for one of them to touch me there. I pushed my knees together hoping to rub away the pain myself. Derek grabbed my knees and forced them apart.*

"Answer me!" Aiden demanded.

"More. I want more." *I went to reach between my legs and make myself cum.*

*Aiden grabbed my wrist before it got close. He took my hand and placed it on his cock over his pants. I massaged him, feeling his thickness. I wanted him inside me. I wanted all three of them inside me. I wanted to know what it felt like to have all of them.*

"Naughty girls don't get to have more." *Aiden took his hand and traced the outside of my pussy.*

"Please," I begged again.

*Jason started kissing my neck. Slowly at first then more aggressively. Derek started laying kisses on my inner thigh. Their mouths against my skin increased the desire, the want, the need.*

"Only good girls get to cum." *Aiden traced my slit still not entering.*

"Fuck," I called out.

Drenched in sweat I looked around. I was in the cell,

alone. I had dreamt that. Shit, what was wrong with me? They held me captive and I was dreaming of them. My heart pounded in my chest.

My pussy throbbed letting me know it didn't give a damn if it was a dream or not. I needed to cum. Not giving a damn who was guarding me I slid my hands down my pants. I was soaked.

My clit was ready, needing to release the tension. I was too soaked. It was hard to get enough friction to orgasm. Shit.

"What are you doing?" one of The Trips asked.

I slightly sat up, still rubbing myself. He wore a suit and a grouchy frown. It was Aiden. Of course it was. At least if it was Derek he would have enjoyed the view or even helped.

"No...none of your business," I stuttered. I was still trying to get off. I needed this.

"I have eyes." He stood and came over to the gate.

He was watching me touch myself. Not that he could actually see it since my hand was in my pants.

"Then...then look away," I stammered.

"Get over here!" he demanded.

I stopped rubbing myself. Getting up I stomped over to the gate and crossed my arms across my chest. "What?"

Aiden slid his hand down my pants. Wasting no time, he went to my clit. "You like that?" He grazed my center.

"Yes," I moaned. I needed him so badly.

"Tell me who's a good girl." He sped up, bringing me closer.

CHAPTER 12

*Aiden and the finger*

I WAITED UNTIL DEREK WALKED KIRA BACK INSIDE before I approached her friend. She was brought here for a specific reason, and I hoped she had actually accomplished that. Yea, she was a hard worker and we were all grateful to have her around, but none of that mattered. It only mattered what she could do for us.

"Hello Sir," she said when I approached her. She had been playing with the new puppy.

"Call me Aiden, please," I sighed. It was annoying how she only called me sir, yet called Jason and Derek by their names.

"Yes, Sir. How can I help you?" She pulled one of her braids away from the puppy who was trying to attack it.

"Did she tell you?" There was no need for small talk.

"No. And before you give me that disappointed father look, it was one conversation. You said Derek would bring her to me daily. I told you it would take time." She picked up the puppy and snuggled him.

"We don't have much time. I told you what would happen to her if she doesn't talk. My family will be here soon and they will not be as nice as I am." I ground my teeth.

76

She snorted. The girl actually snorted through her nose when I said 'nice as me.' There was no way she was implying I wasn't nice. After helping her and pulling her off the streets. I knew what her previous occupation was and that seemed far worse than working for me.

"What is funny about that?" I asked.

"Um, no offense Sir. It's just, well, you aren't nice." She averted her eyes. "Do you not remember how you got me here?"

I remembered. In all honesty, I had thought it went really well. After we had brought Kira back here, we realized quickly she wasn't talking. Jason had suggested we find her family. Someone like Kira was less concerned about self preservation and more concerned with protecting people she loved.

Her friend wasn't easy to find. The people that lived on her alley refused to talk to us. It seemed they had been more eager to give up Kira, than this girl. Finally, Derek used his smooth talking to convince a woman to tell us there was one person Kira gave a damn about and where to find her.

The friend had been working at a rich person's house. The owner was an older married man who had hired her to be with both him and his wife. I'm not one to judge, but what we walked in on was appalling. Both the women were working on the man as he paid no attention to them. He didn't even seem to be enjoying it. Degrading them and calling the friend a list of foul names I refused to even think about. I couldn't figure out why he would pay her just to treat her like trash.

It wasn't my job to interrupt but then the man raised his hand to her. Slapped her right across the face. Blackness covered my vision. I heard the women scream, but ignored them. Jason and Derek had to pull me off of him. Later I learned they got a few hits in as well, but I had been excessive.

Afterward we offered her a job. The only stipulation was

she would have to get Kira to tell us where the bag was that she stole from us.

"Was there anything else sir? She needs to eat." She showed me the puppy who was nipping at her shirt now that she didn't have access to her braids.

"Yea, what is your name again?" There was only one name on my mind lately and I needed to stop thinking about her.

"Vickie. Oh, I do have a question for you, sir." She smiled up at me, her eyes grew wide.

"Again, it's Aiden. Go ahead." I waved her on.

"Is dating allowed? I mean like here at work?" She batted her eyes at me.

Was she hitting on me? She was sweet and all but I had no interest in her. "Look, you are cute, but we should keep this professional."

She laughed and looked at the ground. "Sir, not you. Miguel. I really like him, but I don't want to ruin this job."

"Oh. Yea, go for it." I turned and left before she started asking about him. I hadn't even known there was a worker named Miguel. With so many servants, it was hard to keep track.

Derek was waiting for me at the bottom of the stairs when I went in for my shift to watch Kira. "Sorry, I'm late."

"Which woman is it now?" I laughed. He only ever had one thing on his mind.

"I wish. It's Grandpa. He wants to go over the entertainment for the party." He ran his hand through his hair.

"Better not keep him waiting." I walked past him.

"Yea, you know how he can get. Man can't take a joke." Derek took the stairs two at a time.

I went over to the gate to check on Kira. She was sleeping. The sloth stuffed animal that Pat insisted on was snuggled in her grasp. A soft snore escaped her lips.

When I had thought for a moment that my actions had

killed her, a part of me hurt. It made no sense. Why should I give a damn about her? She hadn't done anything to warrant me caring. Yet, here I was literally watching her sleep.

Another snore. This time it was more raspy. She shifted and turned onto her back. Was she having a nightmare? She gripped the sloth. Kira kicked her legs. Then she rubbed her feet against the mattress.

Should I wake her? I didn't want her in distress.

"Hmmm," she called out.

*Did she just moan?*

She licked her lips.

"Please," she moaned.

My dick instantly got hard.

She was having a sexual dream. There was no other explanation. I wanted to be in that cell. I wanted to be the one she was dreaming about. Grinding my teeth I shoved my hands in my pocket. I would not give in to her.

"Fuck," she called out and opened her eyes.

I backed away from the gate so she wouldn't see me right away. Keeping an eye on her I watched her every move. She shoved her hands down her pants. The blanket was covering her but I knew what she was doing. Fuck. She was gonna make herself cum and there was nothing I could do about it.

Kira squirmed. She was rubbing herself but instead of ecstasy she looked pained. Why? I should have sat in the chair and ignored her. I should have let her do her thing in peace. Instead I watched.

Her hand was in her pants. Her face was pure frustration. I couldn't take it much longer. I wanted to help her. Needed to. All I had to do was help her cum and then I could go back to getting information from her. If she didn't talk to me I was positive at one point she would tell her best friend. Hopefully it would happen before it was too late.

A sigh danced from her lips. She was having so much trouble.

"Get over here!" I demanded.

Startled, she glanced up at me. I was at the gate waiting for her. Slowly she removed her hands from her pants and stared at me. Did she know what I wanted to do to her?

Slowly she got up and walked over to me. "What?"

First, before I helped I needed her permission. "Let me help you."

"How?" she asked. She crossed her arms across her chest.

I looked down at her waist. She knew what I was asking, I just needed her to allow it. She nodded. Yes.

"I'm going to fix this." I slid my hand down her pants.

No underwear of course. My finger quickly found her slit. She was wet. Fuck, so wet. I rubbed her clit. Gentle at first. I was gauging her reaction. She had to want this as badly as I did. Her lips parted.

"You like that?" I asked as she grabbed the bars.

I wanted more of her. All of her. I needed her to beg for more.

"Yes," she moaned.

"Beg," I demanded. I slid my finger inside. She was so tight. Fuck, she felt so good. I wanted my dick inside her.

"Hu...huh?" she stuttered.

"Be a good girl and beg me to let you finish!" I pulled my hand away.

"Seriously?" she gasped.

I took her hand that had been in her pants and brought it to my lips. I licked her pussy juices from her fingers. She panted as I tasted her. Fuck it was heaven. I wanted to drop to my knees and lap up every last drop of her. Nothing had ever tasted sweeter.

"Fine. Can you finish?" she asked.

"You are so naughty. You can do better than that." I put

my hand back in her pants. Close enough to feel her heat, but not close enough to feel her juices.

"Please," she whispered.

"Don't you want this?" I asked, taunting her.

"Yes, please let me cum," she begged.

"That's a good girl." I rubbed my finger against her clit. "I knew you could do it."

I rubbed faster. Hearing her panting undid me. I wanted so badly to take her, all of her. It would be too risky. I couldn't have her, not unless she told me where the fucking bag was. I pushed that thought away, now was not the time.

Her juices ran down my finger as I rubbed. She moaned, allowing me to please her. I slid my middle finger inside of her and rubbed while my thumb continued to rub her clit. She grabbed the bars so tightly I could see the whites of her knuckles. I could see her getting closer.

"Say my name as you come," I demanded.

She tightened her pussy against my finger. She was getting so close. I reached my free hand up her shirt to grab her breasts. Her nipples were perked and ready. I pinched lightly.

"Aiden," she moaned. Her pussy pulsated against my hand.

I removed my hand and licked the juices she had released onto me.

She licked her lips, still panting.

"Stop doing that!" I demanded.

"Doing what," Kira asked. Knowing what I meant, she licked her lips again. Taking a step back from the bars she bit her lip.

"Tell me to stop now!" I growled, stepping into the cell. I had to stop this.

She laughed wholeheartedly exposing her neck.

I grabbed her hair, pulled her into me, and pressed my lips against hers.

"Fuck," I moaned.

Our bodies pressed together. Our tongues intertwined.

My lips pressed into hers. She grabbed my shirt intensifying the kiss.

"You are dangerous," I moaned into her mouth.

"Then stop kissing me." She bit my lip.

We both knew that wouldn't happen. I would kiss her until my last breath. I reached up her shirt and found her breasts again. I played with them as I pushed her against the wall.

I needed to be inside her.

"Why are you doing this?" she pulled her lips from mine.

"What?" It was as if she dumped cold water over me.

"Why? Do you think I'll fuck you and after tell you where the bag is?" she snapped.

*She thought so little of me. She didn't feel our connection.* "Is it working?" I asked, pain laced every word.

She pulled down her shirt and pushed the hand away that was still playing with her nipples. "I hate you," she said and turned away from me.

## CHAPTER 13

*Kira and the library*

I PULLED THE COVERS OVER MY HEAD. AIDEN HADN'T said a word after I told him I hated him. Did I mean it? Maybe. He was the last person I wanted to make me cum like that. And forcing me to beg. I could feel the heat in my cheeks. I enjoyed it. I really had. It was so hot the way he was talking to me.

His fingers felt so good against my pussy. Fuck! I couldn't believe I let him do that. I begged for it. Had he asked for more, I would have given it to him. Yea, I hated him as a person. He was holding me captive. But there was no denying the way he made me cum so easily.

Then the kiss. There was so much unsaid in that kiss. I could still feel his lips against mine. I just needed him to tell me it wasn't because of the bag. I needed to hear that he actually wanted me. He didn't.

Hiding under the covers from him was childish. Hugging the sloth stuffed animal was even more childish. I should have approached him and asked him to fuck me. Come into my cell, bend me over the bed and rail me as hard as he could. I pulled the covers tighter around me, what was I thinking? I never had such nasty thoughts.

It wasn't like I wanted to hold onto my virginity forever, but sex caused problems. Unless you got paid like Vickie did. If you did it for pleasure, it turned into love. And love only led to loss and children. Both were things I wasn't willing to have in my life.

Hours later Aiden was talking to someone else. I hadn't moved and I refused to fall asleep. I didn't need another one of those dreams. Dreaming of those men was what led to Aiden fingering me so deeply that I came all over his fingers. Then he licked it off. Shit, I was getting myself worked up again.

Since I had already dealt with Derek and Aiden today, I assumed Jason was here to guard me. After I knew Aiden was gone I removed the blanket from my head.

Jason sat in the recliner with a glass of red wine and a book. He wore jeans and a brown knit sweater. Taking a sip of his wine he set it on a side table and grabbed a slice of cheese to eat.

I watched him read for a little while without uttering a word. He looked so peaceful. Not that I blamed him, reading was always the best escape. I missed my books. I missed getting lost in a world and forgetting that the real one even existed.

"What are you reading?" I asked. He was so into the book, I had to know.

"It by Stephen King," he answered without looking up.

"Never heard of that." I had read plenty of books growing up and the name and author didn't ring a bell.

"You wouldn't have. It was banned." He closed the book. "Apparently children were too scared of it. So, instead of parents not letting their children read it, they banned the whole thing."

"Well that's crappy," I huffed. I wanted to ask him to let

me read it when he was done. What else was I gonna do while locked up in here. But I didn't. I refused to give these men the satisfaction of me wanting anything from them. Images of Aiden and I danced in my head, well that was a one time thing and wouldn't happen again.

"So, what are your hobbies?" he asked as if he could read the boredom across my face.

"I steal. You know that. Hence why I'm here." I rolled my eyes.

"That's a job, not a hobby." He leaned closer to the gate. "What do you do when you aren't stealing from people?"

Have I ever been asked that? I didn't think so. Yea, Vickie and I talked about stuff like that, but that was it. When my mother was alive she refused to acknowledge anything but living from one day to the next. What she did was far from living.

"I refuse to believe you are only capable of stealing." He took a long drink from his wine glass.

As if on cue one of his servants came and refilled his glass. Easy for him to talk about hobbies when he had people waiting on him.

"I read. When I can. There isn't much time left for much else." Surviving took up most of my free time.

"The average person has three hobbies," he said matter of factly.

"Yea, so what are yours?" I asked.

"Reading, tech, and learning odd facts." He took another bite of cheese.

"So tell me some facts." I hugged the sloth.

"Okay. Sloths eat, fuck, and sleep. That's about it for them. A group of ravens is called an unkindness. The brain is mostly fat. Um, and you can't lick your own elbow." He took another sip of his wine.

Maybe it was because my brain was all fat, but I tried to lick my elbow. I couldn't. Jason saw this and started laughing. A full belly hyena laugh. It reminded me of the laugh Derek made when he was getting his dick sucked. Pushing aside that thought I laughed too.

"Told ya. Random facts." He opened his book back up.

I flopped back on the bed slightly embarrassed. Talking with him was a great distraction for a few moments. I didn't want him to read his book. I wanted him to continue talking to me. His words were smooth and fun. Those few moments of conversation were welcome in a sea of hectic crazy life I had gotten myself into.

"Do you want a book or something?" Jason looked up from the book he had been reading.

Intrigued, I asked. "Do I get to pick?"

"Of course, I'll bring you to the library."

"Won't your brothers get mad?" I snapped. It wasn't fair to lash out at him when he was being nice. I knew that, but I still hated being locked up.

Jason shrugged and took the keys from his pocket.

I jumped up immediately. Way too happy to get my pick of a book. I was going to grab the thickest one I could find. Or maybe he would let me grab more than one.

He ran over to me and placed his arm around me. "Slow down, you are still injured."

I let him guide me from the cell and up the stairs. As much as I wanted to walk on my own, he was right. My back still ached. The pain was getting to me.

Jason brought me back to the library I had met him in. It seemed like so long ago when I was here. I was free then and planning on stealing from them. I had sat on that comfy chair in the corner getting lost in a book.

It was then that I had contemplated staying. I had thought

of actually being one of their servants. How different would things have been had I? I wouldn't be their prisoner. Life would have remained simple. Shit, had I made the wrong choice?

"Pick out any you want." Jason waved his hands.

"Any? Like more than one?" I bounced on my heels.

"Yes. As many as you would like." He still had his arm around me.

I turned into him. He was so close I could feel his breath against my lips. The smell of the wine he had drunk earlier lingered in the air. I knew it was wrong to want him. That didn't matter.

I needed him. I pushed up on my toes bringing my lips to his.

"Fuck," he moaned.

His arms were around me pulling me into him. My stomach flipped. His kiss tasted like going home. His warmth made me feel safe.

The longer we were kissing, the more I fell into him. His kiss was greedy as if he needed it as much as I did. Everything faded away. It was only us. My hands gripped his hair pulling him deeper into me.

He pulled away. I almost let out a pout. What the heck? I couldn't figure out why he did that. We were enjoying each other. I knew he was enjoying me. I could feel it.

"I can't," he panted.

"Fine," I snapped. There was no need for an explanation. He didn't want to tell me, fine. He could do whatever he wanted. It was terrible to even want him. I shouldn't have kissed him.

"I want to. Trust me. I do." He ran his thumb along his bottom lip. "I want to lick every inch of you until you are undid by my touch."

Fuck, my pussy fluttered.

He started pacing. "If you just tell us where the bag is, things will be fine."

"Of course," I sighed. Everything kept coming back to that damn bag.

"I don't care why you took it. Everyone has their reasons for why they do things. It's just, we need it back." His voice growled on the last words.

"Right, you guys need anything? No." I turned and went to the nearest book shelf.

"Just grab some books and let's go. I'm not gonna argue with you." He turned and waited by the door.

I didn't even check the titles. I grabbed the first five books I saw. It didn't matter if they were good or not. They would be a much needed distraction from all of this.

All I wanted was to get out of here. Grab Vickie. Sell the bag and be gone. Kissing Jason and getting fingered by Aiden didn't change any of that.


For the next few days I stayed in my cell. The Triplets tried to talk to me. Well, Derek and Jason did. I ignored them. They all had me mesmerized for a moment. I couldn't let that happen again.

They had even brought Vickie down to my cell. She tried to talk to me. It took everything in me to ignore her. I had to. She would have convinced me to give up the bag. To stay here. Part of me wanted to. It would have been easier. I couldn't do that. Vickie and I needed a better life even if she didn't realize it.

Pat even tried talking to me. He was so nice and I considered him as close to a friend as anyone had been except Vickie. He would bring my food in and ramble about how great life could be here. I wouldn't even look up from my book to pay attention.

I stayed reading. The books transported me to different worlds. I devoured them. Pretending to be the people in the novels. It was easy to pretend my life wasn't real.

## CHAPTER 14

## *Kira and the talk*

SOMEONE CAME BARRELING DOWN THE STAIRS. Their footsteps sounded like a bulldozer taking down a house. I kept reading my book. Whatever was going on was none of my business.

"Open the gate!" Vickie's small voice sounded loud for once.

I did not want to see her.

The gate slid open. I kept my face in my book refusing to look up at her.

My book was ripped from my hands and tossed across the room.

Vickie and Pat stood there. Both had scowls on their faces and their arms crossed. With the uniform they looked like angry bumble bees.

I took the blanket, put it over my head and rolled to the side.

That too was ripped from my grasp.

"Get up!" Vickie snapped. She didn't yell, like ever. It wasn't in her. As long as I had known her she had never raised her voice.

Maybe it was the way she yelled at me, or the fact that she yelled at me at all. Maybe it was because I was being a shitty friend to her. Whatever the reason, I got up. I was sluggish from having spent so much time in bed.

Vickie linked her arm in mine and Pat grabbed my other side. After a weird side shuffle they whisked me out of the cell and up the basement stairs. I glanced back to see who had been watching me but I wasn't sure. It was one of the triplets but with only seeing their face, I didn't know which one it was.

They brought me outside into the backyard with the beautiful landscapes. The puppy from the other day bunny hopped over to me. His ears flopped in the wind and I was afraid he would be taken away like a feather. I bent down and gave him some love.

I knew Vickie and Pat wanted to talk, but I was putting it off for a few more minutes at least. Whatever it was it felt heavy and I wasn't ready for it.

"We need to talk," Vickie said. Her voice was back to her soft fairy sounds.

"I figured." I picked up the puppy and sat on the nearest bench.

"I want to stay here." She turned away from me.

There was so much in what she had said. Earlier when we had talked about it she had mentioned as much, but this felt different. It felt final.

"Why?" I snapped. Everything I had done was to get us out of here.

"It's a good life. The Trips aren't so bad. The work is easy. There are great people here." She waved at Pat.

"The Trips are terrible. They have held me captive. I almost died under their care. Here we will never be free. Pat is the only good thing here." I ground my teeth. Vickie had always had it worse than me on the streets. Of course to her this was easy.

91

"The Trips are good people, Sweetie. I keep telling you that. You have to give them a chance." Pat placed his hand on my shoulder. "They haven't been that bad to you have they?"

Visions of Aiden's hand in my pants flashed across my mind. At that moment he hadn't been so bad. Then there was the kiss with Jason. There was so much in that kiss, I wanted more.

"What is it? Your face is beat red." Vickie sat beside me.

"Okay, but you two must promise not to say anything." I took a deep breath.

They both nodded.

"I kinda kissed Jason and um Aiden sorta fingermetill-Imeltedintoapuddle." The last part came out so fast it was one jumbled mess.

"Oh, Sweetie. I knew it. The way they look at you. And when you were sick the way Aiden worried about you." Pat clasped his hands together. "This is so great."

"Woah, you did what?" Vickie waved her hand. "You don't need to repeat the last part. I get it. Then why all this angst?"

"They are keeping me captive!" I snapped. Had they forgotten about that part?

"Cause you won't tell them where the bag you stole is." Vickie got up and stood in front of me. "For whatever reason it's super important to them."

"Sweetie, you may not know what you stole, but trust me. It's mega important. Not just to them." Pat stood next to Vickie.

"But...but...If I give it back, we will never get the money to go to Mexico. We will be stuck in New Boston." I set the puppy back on the ground. He gave my sweatpants a little nip before running away.

"I met someone." Vickie knelt in front of me. "I won't leave him."

My stomach dropped. The Triplets had fooled around with me. Were they doing the same with her? Did I have a right to be jealous? No. Could it have been Derek? He hadn't done anything with me. It could have been all three. She said someone. Maybe it was only one of them. Ugh, my stomach twisted. Vomit crept up my throat.

"Who?" I asked. I had to know even if it hurt. Knowing I had no rights to them and was still trying to hate them, didn't matter.

"His name is Miguel. He works here. I can't wait for you to meet him." Vickie grabbed my hands.

"Oh." I let out a long deep breath. "So why does it matter to both of you if I give them the bag?"

"We care about you, Sweetie. The Trips don't want to do this to you. Their family is coming in soon. If they find out you stole the bag, they will have you killed. Sure they will put on a fake trial. In the end you will be found guilty and they will kill you. No one wants that." Pat wiped a tear from his eye.

I stood and paced. My life mattered to me. Could I really give it up for some dream of Mexico? Dying wouldn't help anyone. Even if Vickie wanted to stay, they might go after her next. If I wasn't alive to sell the bag to Carlos none of it would matter anyway. This would all be for nothing.

Vickie stared at me with pleading eyes. She wanted to stay. Mexico would be nothing without her. If this was what she truly wanted then I would give it to her.

Pat had a few more rogue tears. I barely knew him, yet he had instantly become a friend. He cried for me. My life mattered to him. I couldn't hurt my two true friends.

"Fine. I'll do it," I whispered.

They grabbed me from both sides. The hug hurt the lingering pains in my back. It didn't matter. I squeezed back.

These two people were my family. If they wanted me to give back the stupid bag then that's what I would do.

"Let's go," Pat released me and grabbed my hand.

"Now? We are going to tell them now?" I asked. I didn't know why, but I thought I had a little time to tell them. Maybe let them beg for it like Aiden made me beg to cum.

"No. I mean you can, but we are taking you to your new room." Vickie grabbed my other hand.

"Huh?" I stopped.

"Well, Pat convinced the Trips to upgrade your living quarters. Part of us bringing you out here was so they could get it ready." Vickie gleamed. "You are gonna love it."

"One condition on all this," I said.

They both turned to me. Pat had tears filling in his eyes again. Vickie swallowed hard.

"I tell them when I'm ready. I just wanna mess with them a little bit longer. They have kept me prisoner for a while. They deserve it." I smiled.

"You wanna tease them. Ha. I love it. Those boys are no match for you," Vickie laughed.

"Sweetie, you don't have much time. The family will be here soon. You wanna mess with them I won't stop you. Just remember if they don't have it before the family arrives then you are dead. That's something I can't handle." Pat wiped another tear from his eyes.

"Deal, now let's go." I stepped forward.

For the first time in a while, I belonged. These were my friends. The Trips and I may have had a complicated relationship, but that was something I was willing to work on. I was drawn to them there was no denying that anymore. At least I didn't have to deny it anymore. I would give them back the bag and ask them to stay on.

I would even wear the stupid uniform, not the pigtails. There was only so much I would be willing to do. Did I think they would forgive me and let me stay, maybe. It was a risk I was willing to take for Vickie and Pat.

It was amazing how quickly I turned things around. One minute I was hell bent on escaping and selling their precious bag. The next, I was figuring out how to convince them to let me stay.

Within a few minutes of navigating this mansion we were outside of a room that if I was correct was close to the library. Had they really moved me close to the library? If they had then I would kiss each one of them. Maybe.

Pat opened the door.

It was beautiful.

Gray and silver wallpaper lined the walls. A mahogany bed with lacy canopy curtains lay in the middle. One wall, and I mean the entire wall was covered with shelves. I immediately went over. Hundreds of books were crammed on the book cases. Tears swelled in my eyes. Another door was near the bed that was opened to a private bathroom. The sloth I had cuddled sat on a black bedding set.

There was a nightstand with a lamp and the books from my cell. The rug was fluffy and had the lines in it from a vacuum cleaner. The entire room was pristine. There was no way it was mine.

A servant bopped in and set a tray with fruit and wine on the bed. I opened my mouth to thank her but nothing came out. It was nicer than anything I had imagined. When I thought of a different life I thought of a tiny room with a bed and kitchenette in it. Not this.

My suspicions crept up. The Triplets didn't know I was planning on giving them the bag. Why did they do this for me?

As if on cue, all three walked in.

I grabbed a few grapes and chucked them at them.

"Hey, what's that for?" Derek ducked and laughed at me.

"What's this for?" I tossed a strawberry at Jason.

"Calm down," Vickie and Pat said simultaneously.

"Yea, what's your problem?" Jason asked.

"What is your problem?" I tossed another piece of fruit at him.

"We are trying to be nice," Derek laughed.

"Why?" I screamed. It made no sense.

"Not really sure." Aiden shrugged.

"Then why do it?" I tossed a grape at Aiden.

He plucked it out of the air and tossed it in his mouth. Ugh he was such a cocky bastard.

"I told you they are good people, Sweetie." Pat grabbed my hand before I could toss any more food.

"Bullshit," I scoffed.

"Okay, that's enough." Aiden waved his hand. "Like it or not you are staying here now. We couldn't stand seeing you in that cold basement cell. Besides, if you don't talk soon you are gonna die, so we wanted to make your last few days comfortable."

I opened my mouth to tell them I would talk. I went to spill the beans about where the bag was. I tried. The words got stuck in my throat. Maybe it was my pride that wouldn't let me speak.

Aiden turned and left the room. Vickie and Pat went to stay, but he beckoned them to leave. Both of them gave me a pleading puppy dog look before they walked out. Jason followed them.

Derek went over to a recliner in the corner and took a seat. He popped the lever and the chair leaned back. He eyed me as he removed his hoodie leaving himself in just gray sweatpants and a white tank top.

I licked my lips before taking a sip of the wine. Now there were no bars between us. *This new setup may not be so bad after all.*

## CHAPTER 15

## *Kira and the slap*

HOT WATER FLOWED OVER MY SKIN. THE SHOWER had two heads and both had the best pressure I had ever experienced. My hair and body had already been washed. There was even a razor on the counter that I used.

When I went into the bathroom I hadn't expected much. I would seriously have to start changing my expectations for these men. There was a hygiene care kit on the counter. Shampoo, conditioner, toothbrush, some sea salt scrub thing, and a brand new razor were among some of the items. A few others looked foreign to me and the wax looked painful.

I took my time indulging in all the things I had never gotten to experience. Once I was done I stood there letting the water erase my pain. This was a different life. This was my wish I had made on my birthday all those days ago. Well if I could forget that I was being held captive and I would never make it to Mexico.

There was also the little problem of The Triplets. I would tell them where the bag was and then I would have to hope they would let me stay. In the meantime I wanted to see how far I could push them. The thoughts of Aiden's touch and Jason's lips were driving me insane.

I wanted more of them. Shit, who was I kidding, I needed more of them.

Once my fingertips were pruned, I finally got out of the shower. They even had a heated towel rack. They really had more money than they knew what to do with. If I ignored the many people living on the streets, I could get used to this.

Not that I could ever ignore that. If they did let me stay, I would find a way to help the homeless. Maybe I could do some good in this new found situation.

Stepping out of the bathroom I went into my new room in just a towel. The clothes I had been in stunk like the cell I was in so there was no way I was putting those back on. Yes, I used to live next to a dumpster, but in a place like this I didn't have to stink. If there were no clothes for me, I would be content with sleeping like this. I had never slept naked and the idea excited me.

Derek was dozed off in the chair. He wasn't much of a guard. I could have snuck right past him and left. If it wasn't for the deal I made with Vickie I would have considered leaving.

"Wha...huh...I," he mumbled as he stirred awake.

"It's just me. Do you have any clothes for me?" I batted my eyes at him.

He pulled his white tank top off and tossed it at me. "Not that I want to clothe you, but your wish is my command."

I wanted to lick every inch of his perfect body. He looked like a god from the books I used to read, or a fallen angel. Yea, a fallen angel was a better description. I grabbed the tank top and put it on, fully aware he was watching me.

"So, you like your new digs?" He sat up in his chair.

"Yea, it's better than being locked up in a damn cell." I dropped the towel and sat on the bed.

"How about the fact that there are no bars between us?" He winked at me.

Was he taunting me? Did he know how badly I wanted him? Did he know I dreamed of him? Well, him and his brothers.

"What does that mean?" I bit my lip.

"Oh Babe, you know exactly what I mean." He got up and approached me.

He put his hands on either side of me on the bed. His body was so close to mine. I could reach out and lick him. Instead I leaned back. My back hit the soft bed. Great, I was laying down and he was hovering over me.

"See, nothing between us now," he purred. "All you have to do is reach out and touch me."

"An...And...um...why would I do that?" I scooted back.

This is what I wanted. I knew that. I had dreamt of his hands on mine. I imagined what it would be like to be with him. To feel his skin against mine. Now that he was so close I was scared. I had fooled around with a few guys, but that was it.

"I see how you look at me. Shit, you look at all of us like you can't wait to strip us down. You wanna fuck me, I can tell." Derek grinned.

My hand made contact with his face before I realized what I had done. I slapped him. Shit. On impulse I pulled him into me and squeezed.

"I'm so sorry." I stroked his hair.

"It's all good. You hit like a girl." He rubbed his face into my neck.

I pushed him away. "Very funny."

"So are you gonna admit it?" He licked his lips inches from my face.

He was right. I wanted him. I wanted him to take me right there. All I had to do was say the words. He was so close and ready. All that separated his dick from my pussy was a pair of gray sweatpants. My hips flexed forward. I rubbed against him.

"Good enough for me." He pushed his hard cock against me.

I tried to open my mouth to speak. His lips were on mine before I could open them. Like Jason his kiss consumed me. Unlike him, his was playful. He bit my lip and deepened the kiss.

As our tongues collided he grinded against me. I wrapped my legs around him forcing him to be as close to me without entering me. Rolling my hips I directed my pussy right against his cock. He was so ready and so damn big. Had he not had on his pants he would have been inside me.

His hand moved up my shirt to my chest. His thumb grazed my nipple, sending a chill through my body. I moaned, trying to beg for him. I couldn't speak with his frantic kissing. His other hand grabbed my ass, squeezing it.

Aside from the white tank top I was naked. It still felt like I was wearing too many clothes. I wanted my skin against his. I needed to feel all of him.

A tingle started in my pussy. Small at first, barely noticeable. As he continued to grind against me the tingle expanded. My pussy throbbed for him.

Too soon. I was already about to explode. I didn't want to cum before he was inside me. A simple rub wasn't enough for me. I needed all of him.

Pulling my lips from his I panted, "Wait, I'm so close. I want you inside me."

"Oh Baby, you think I'm stopping with one orgasm?" He grinded into me harder with more intensity. He lifted his head back and laughed. The same laugh he had when that woman was blowing him, but this time there was an intensity in his eyes. A desire that wasn't there with her.

"But, I've never..." I tried to say I never had multiple orgasms, but the electricity ran through me.

"Let go, let it happen," Derek purred.

Dances erupted around my body. A lust of pure electricity vibrated through me. I dug my nails into him and pulled him closer. He kissed me covering my moans. When the last of the eruption left my body he scooped me up and set me further onto the bed.

He grabbed the shirt I was wearing and ripped it down the center exposing all of me. Derek pulled down his gray sweatpants that now had a wet spot all over the front. I bit my lip, that was me all over his pants.

His cock was at my entrance before I could process it. He rubbed the tip against it, getting it wet, so wet. I rolled my hips into him begging him to slide his cock inside.

"Wait, um..." I tried to think. Vickie told me about this moment. Told me not to be stupid about it. "Protection."

He rammed his cock inside me without a condom. He filled all of me. The rawness intoxicated me. I tried to protest, but fuck it was incredible. His cock didn't move, he stayed inside me doing nothing. I bucked my hips to get him to fuck me.

Derek slid his dick out of me. I huffed in complaint. "I needed to know what that felt like without one." Derek pulled a condom from his sweatpants pocket and slid it on.

Fuck. He entered me again. Slower this time. The difference of the condom was subtle and only slightly annoying. He rocked back and forth inside me. I quickly adjusted to the size. Had he not rammed it in me I didn't think it would ever fit.

"Well how does it feel?" I asked. Insecurity laced my question. I wanted to make sure he was enjoying it as much as I was.

"Like coming home." He kissed me.

Our bodies were intertwined. I felt every pulsation. Never

had I been so aware of myself. Every touch from him lit a fire. Sweat dripped as our bodies became one. He was right, this was coming home. Love was a concept I didn't believe in, but this had to be close to it.

He would go slow and deep. Every time his dick hit my deepest parts I let out a moan. Closer. He pushed again. Closer. He pushed deeper. Closer.

"I'm..." I ground into him.

"That's it. Cum for me, Baby." He rammed his dick inside.

I exploded.

My entire body shook as I came on Derek's cock.

He fucked me until the last of the shakes stopped.

Once I caught my breath he put his arm under me and rolled us on the bed. Now I was on top of him. I wasn't really sure what to do. I sat up some and ground into him. It was good, but seemed a little off.

"Like this." He pushed me completely upright and grabbed my hands.

I let out a squeal. He was so deep inside me I could barely move.

He put my hands on his chest and grabbed my hips. Derek moved me for him. After a few minutes we found a rhythm. I rode him. While bouncing on his cock I tilted my head back. Sweat dripped down my chest. My body belonged to him.

I didn't hear the door open.

Someone else's hand intertwined in my hair.

One of the other trips yanked my head back so I would look in his eyes.

I didn't stop riding.

"You like that?" he asked as he pushed me further onto his brother.

"Yes," I moaned.

I didn't know which brother it was, nor did I care.

Chances were it wasn't Jason. He didn't share like the other two did. I wished I could have all three of them, but for now these two would do.

The other triplet, probably Aiden, kissed me. It was soft yet demanding. He continued to push me onto his brother as I rode Derek.

"That's it, Baby," Derek moaned.

I rode Derek deeper while kissing him. Derek pulsated beneath me. He panted heavier. I was pretty sure he was getting close to coming.

"You gonna let my brother cum?" the other triplet asked.

I nodded.

"Say it!" he demanded.

"Yes, I'm gonna let him cum." Ripples ran through my body. I was so close.

Derek bucked into me, pulling my hips further down onto him. He pulsated inside me as I exploded around him. Together we came with the guidance of the other triplet.

I looked up to kiss him again when the door flew open hitting the wall.

The third triplet. Stood there in a suit with a blue tie. There was no mistaking the smug look on his face. Aiden. Which meant...

"Jason, you seem to be enjoying yourself." Aiden walked into the room and slapped his brother on the back. "About time."

## CHAPTER 16

## *Aiden and the offer*

"DID YOU TWO MANAGE TO FUCK THE INFORMATION out of her?" I sat at my desk.

"Jealous?" Derek leaned back in the chair across from me.

Damn straight I was jealous. Seeing them with her made me want to join in. The ways we could all please her made my dick hard. I wanted her wriggling underneath all of us. I wanted her begging, like she begged me earlier.

"You two share women all the time. I have fun for once and you are all pissy," Jason snapped.

"This woman is different." I stood and slammed the desk. She was different in more ways than one.

"No shit," Derek scoffed.

"Back to the point. Did she tell you anything?" I didn't want to talk about how different she was. The way she felt when I touched her. How her face glowed when she came. Her lips against mine. How in that moment I would have given her the world.

Even without that I knew I wanted her. When her stubborn ass was in the tub on the verge of death and I scooped her out. My heart raced as I wrapped her in my arms. I never wanted to let her go.

Watching my brothers with her let me know they felt the same way about her.

"No." Jason dragged his hand across his face.

"So what do we do? Grandpa will be here tomorrow, and the party is the day after." I ground my teeth.

"No, that's next week." Derek stood. He had set up the entertainment so he should know, but he didn't. Not that I was surprised. He treated life like a joke and only thought with his dick.

"Check your phone. I linked my calendar with you." Jason pulled his phone out of his pocket.

Pat sauntered into the office. He had a stack of papers in his hand and a smile plastered across his face. He must have gotten laid recently.

"Hey, Bosses. So, she told you right?" He smiled and set the papers on the desk. "Now, that that's out of the way. I have some papers that need signatures. I have hired everyone for the new estate. It needs a name. Oh and Carlos is still trying to undermine you guys in Forlake Estate."

"That fucking snake!" Derek punched the wall. Left a damn hole in it. His temper wasn't misplaced but it was my office.

"Calm down. Carlos isn't getting shit from us. He can try and buy Forlake, but he doesn't have that kind of money or resources." I glanced at the papers Pat brought in.

"Bosses, I totally get it. But I don't trust that jerk breaker loser. He is trying to buy out New Boston. And what if he finds out about the new project. I just couldn't. Do you know how many people you guys are about to help?" Pat fanned himself.

"Yes, Pat, we know. Wait, why did you say she told us?" Jason asked.

"She told Vickie and I she was gonna tell you guys." Pat waved his hand in the air like this was common knowledge.

"Interesting. Pat, could you tell her we would like to see her in my office." I put the papers in the drawer. "I'll get these signed and a name for you soon."


Half an hour later the door opened. Kira stood there biting her lip. That was the first thing I noticed. Then I realized what she was wearing. Kira had a flowy black mini skirt on with a pink skin tight shirt. Even with all of that, that wasn't what made my dick rock hard. She had her hair in pigtails. She did it on purpose. She purposely did that to her hair. She was taunting me and fuck it was working.

"You are a naughty girl." I leaned on the desk. "Get over here and bend over my desk. My brothers and I need to punish you."

She giggled.

I was captivated by her. The fact that she didn't listen and just stood there made me want her more. I needed to taste her. *Fuck, stop thinking with your dick!* "Where is the bag?"

"Huh. I was hoping to mess with you guys for a little while longer." She dropped her arms by her side. "It's in a brick behind my dumpster. I'll take you guys there in the morning. Now, do I get to be with all three of you or what?"

We all stared at her. She was giving us what we wanted. There was no denying what we all wanted. Even Jason would share with us.

She walked over and grabbed a pen from my desk. Jason and Derek watched her with lust in their eyes. Was this really about to happen? My dick rubbed against my jeans. Now that we knew where the Nant-bots were, we could enjoy her, all of her.

She stood there chewing on my pen cap. "Are you gonna say anything?" She placed her hand on her hip. "Well?" She snapped.

I grabbed her by her waist and set her on my desk. Her wicked smile teased me.

Jason and Derek watched me as I lifted her skirt. She leaned back allowing me access. There was already a wet spot on her panties. I wanted to slide my dick inside of her immediately. Being buried deep inside her was exactly what I needed. Not yet though. I wanted to taunt her first.

I set her skirt back down. She scrunched up her face at me. *Yea, I don't know what I'm doing either.* To add insult I pulled her off the desk. Ugh. What was I doing? This wasn't like me. Ever.

When I was young my parents were always around. They were deeply in love. Their bedroom door would be locked in the middle of the day. We all knew what they were up to. Looking back on it I realized how rare it was to have that kind of love. It was part of why they spent all their time traveling together. Their forever honeymoon.

As I got older I wanted that. Instead I buried myself in my work. Owning half of New Boston wasn't easy. My grandfather started it when he was young. He bought one apartment complex and turned it into a mansion for a rich family. With that profit he kept buying up properties. It was a lucrative business that I was good at. All I was missing was someone to share it with.

Sure I fucked plenty of women. Most of which I shared with Derek. There was something about both of us pleasing a woman that made the whole experience so much better. For a while I thought that was enough. Then that woman walked into my office. Now all I thought about was her. All I wanted was her. I wanted the same love my parents had.

"We need to talk." I backed away from her.

"I told you where the bag was. What's the issue?" She crossed her arms. Hurt filled her eyes. "Do you not want me?"

"That's the problem. I want you." I shoved my hands in my pockets.

"I was giving myself to you. All three of you." She pointed at Jason and Derek.

"We didn't just move you to the new room to be nice." Jason jumped into the conversation. He knew what I was getting at. We all felt the same way about her.

"No shit. It was for me to talk. I did." Kira started walking toward the door. "This was a bad idea. I'm sorry. I shouldn't have thrown myself at you guys."

"Stop right there. You stubborn asshole. We are trying to talk to you," I snapped. This was hard enough to say without her interrupting me.

"Sit your ass down and listen!" Derek demanded.

To my surprise, she listened. Kira sat on the chair and remained silent.

"As I was saying. No, it wasn't to get you to talk. Had Pat and Vickie not convinced you, we would have dealt with the consequences, somehow. Anyway..." Shit, why was this so hard to say. "We want you to stay."

Kira sucked her teeth. She sat there staring at us for a few minutes. I hated not knowing what she was thinking. I had thought she felt the same way about us. Maybe she just wanted to fuck us and leave.

Vickie had told us about her plans to head to Mexico. Was that still what she wanted? It couldn't be. She was ours!

"Okay, I'll stay." Kira raised her arms and dropped them. "I just ask that I clean the library. Cooking isn't my strong suit."

"Huh?" Derek asked. "What are you talking about?"

"We aren't asking you to clean or cook." Jason scrunched up his face.

"We are asking you to stay." I drew in a deep long breath. "With us."

"W...with..you...g...guys?" she asked.

"Yes. All three of us." I stood in front of her. "We all have feelings for you. There are just a few things we need to straighten out."

"What things? I mean yes, I want all three of you. But what things need to be straightened out?" She sucked her teeth again.

"First, you don't date anyone but us." I held up one finger.

She tilted her head back and laughed. "Easy, how could I want for more than you three?"

"Good. In turn we won't date or fuck anyone else." I looked at Derek who nodded. "Now the important part. Our grandfather is coming in tomorrow and the day after we are having an anniversary party for our grandparents. It is also where he will announce his retirement and give us the business. You are to not tell anyone where you come from. Your name will be Kira Jones and you are from the Elites in Tentokesee. It's two countries over if you didn't know that."

"So a poor homeless girl that stole from you isn't good enough for your family?" Her question was filled with bitterness.

"No, it's not. They wouldn't allow it and our Grandfather wouldn't give us the business." There was no point in lying to her.

"It's for two days. After that you can go back to the bitchy homeless girl we all want to rail." Derek wiggled his eyebrows at her.

"Anything else?" she asked.

"No. That's it. You play the part for two days and then you get to have us all to yourself." I smiled. She was ours.

"Two days. How am I gonna act like some elite?" She bit her lip.

"Pat will coach you." Jason chimed in. To have Jason included made it complete.

"Good. Now can we have some fun." I grabbed her hand and pulled her toward the door.

Within a minute we were in her bedroom. I had been dying for a moment like this. I picked her up and set her on the bed. She giggled. Even her laugh was naughty. I couldn't wait to punish her.

Derek mumbled something about supplies and ran from the room. He wouldn't be long. I could have waited for him, but I was growing impatient.

I removed my tie and held it between my hands. "Wanna play a game?"

"What game?" She wiggled.

"We blindfold you and you guess which one of us is eating you." I grinned.

She nodded.

I wrapped the tie around her eyes. After checking to make sure she couldn't see anything I stripped off her clothes. She was a goddess. Every inch of her was perfection. I wanted to kiss every inch of her. She was ours.

Derek returned with a small container and a feather. Oh, he meant business with her. He unscrewed the lid and handed it to Jason. Honey dust. A sensual sweet powder that was placed on the body with a feather. Then of course it's licked off.

We had used it once on another woman before. Now, I hated that. Hated that anything happened before her.

Kira squirmed on the satin sheets. She rubbed her legs together and lifted her hips to me.

Jason dipped the feather in the honey dust. As he stroked her skin with it she moaned.

"Want more?" I whispered.

"Yes," she begged.

"Then you shouldn't be so naughty," I grinned. We all knew she would be getting more. So much more.

## CHAPTER 17

# Kira and the game

"WHAT GAME?" I STAYED ON THE BED LIKE I WAS told. My heart raced, my pussy throbbed.

"We blindfold you and you guess which one of us is eating you." Aiden licked his lips.

I nodded.

Aiden wrapped his tie around my eyes. I couldn't see anything. A chill ran up my spine. *Was I really doing this? Yes.* My every fantasy about these men was about to come true. For a moment in Aiden's office I had thought they didn't want me. My heart had been crushed. I had already decided to take off. Go back to my old life. Then they asked me to stay. Stay with them. It was heaven.

My clothes were removed. It was done quickly and efficiently. Unlike when Derek ripped my shirt. I didn't know which one did it and I didn't care.

Cool air grazed my skin. No, it was soft. Fingertips? No softer than that. Something else caressed my thigh. I couldn't figure out what it was but it left tingles in its wake. I moaned.

"Want more?" Aiden whispered. At least I thought it was him.

"Yes," I begged.

"Then you shouldn't be so naughty," he said.

"Maybe you should teach me a lesson," I shot back.

"Oh we will," Derek laughed. I assumed it was him.

Something wet ran across my thigh. A tongue. Fuck. I was already soaked. There was no way I was going to get through this. It was sweet, sensual torture and it had just begun.

"Time to play," Aiden said.

This one took his time. Going slowly, taunting, teasing. His tongue would graze my clit, barely. He gently blew on my pussy, sending tingles through me. Each time his tongue caressed my slit it barely touched.

I bucked against him, begging for more.

"Want more," he whispered.

"Jason?" I gasped.

"Good girl," he replied. He dragged his tongue forcefully along my slit, then stopped.

I reached between my legs to force his head back down. He was gone. Hands grabbed mine and forced them above my head.

"Next," a low voice said.

He bit the inside of my thigh making his way to my center. I needed him. I wanted so badly to cum. Another bite.

"Please," I begged.

He slid a finger inside me and laughed.

I rolled my hips begging him to finger me until I came.

"Derek?" I moaned.

"Wrong. Naughty girl. Time to be punished." Aiden licked me.

He sucked my clit roughly, bringing me so close to the edge. A hand came down to stop my hips from pushing into his face. His finger slid in and out of me. So close.

Ripples started. I couldn't catch my breath. He licked hard and fast. So close.

Then nothing. His mouth was gone along with his finger.

"Fuck!" I yelled.

They held me down but didn't touch me. Nothing. I squirmed trying to get out of their grasp. I needed to cum. I was so close.

The ripples faded. Tingles stopped. My near explosion was gone.

"Ready for more?" Aiden asked.

"I need to cum," I panted.

"Soon Baby, soon." A hand cupped my face.

The next guy went fast. Diving for my center. Licking hard and fast.

I gasped.

His lips pressed against my clit and he blew a raspberry. It sent vibrations through me. Only one of them would tease me and be playful at the same time.

I laughed and moaned, "Derek."

"Good girl." Derek continued sending me closer.

"This time it's gonna be tricky," Aiden purred.

A thick wet tongue ran along my clit. I moaned and bucked against it. As that tongue went to work, teeth grazed my thigh working its way up to my center.

"Two? That's not fair," I moaned.

"When did we say we were fair?" Aiden whispered in my ear.

Lips touched my breasts. My nipples perked. His teeth teased me. The other two were between my legs working on my pussy. All three men had their mouths on me. I could barely breathe. The ripples came back hard and fast.

A finger slid inside me. I couldn't concentrate on just one of them. Pulses ran through me. My heart slammed in my chest as I got close. Fuck. I was on the cliff. Hands massaged my legs pushing me to the edge of the cliff.

I was about to fall off. I knew they would catch me. I

called out for them. They licked harder. Rubbed. Caressed. Nipped. My body was on fire.

"Yes!" I screamed falling off the edge.

I lost my balance. They were there. The orgasm was strong and hard. I panted while they planted kisses along my skin.

"Good girl," Aiden removed the blindfold. "Ready for more?"

That's exactly what they gave me. So much more. They sent me over the edge multiple times. All four of our bodies intertwined. Somehow we all made it work. I had thought they would take turns. Nope. They all were on me. They rotated teasing me, but they all had part of them on me or in me.

By the time we were finished I couldn't move. I couldn't breathe. My body hurt, but fuck it felt good. I loved every second of it.

When we were finished Jason scooped me up in his arms and brought me to the tub. Derek had already filled it with water. Jason set me in the water. The warmth engulfed me. Aiden grabbed a loofa and washed me down.

After the ache was worked from my body they dried me off and set me in the bed. I had asked for something to sleep in so Derek picked up his shirt from the floor and put it on me. His scent was woody, like he had spent part of the day by a campfire. I breathed it in, letting it put me to sleep.

I woke up and rolled over. The bed was empty. *What had I expected? Them to all sleep in the bed with me? Yes, I expected something more than to wake up alone.* Especially after that night we had.

This would have to be discussed with them. Either they would find a bed big enough for all of us or they would be rotating who slept in bed with me. Waking up alone wasn't an option. I didn't like it one bit.

The door opened. Pat scampered in with a tray. "Hey Sweetie, I brought breakfast." He set the tray on the end of the bed. Eggs, bacon, oatmeal, fresh fruit, and a glass of orange juice was laid out for me.

"Thank you." I sat up and went right for the bacon. It was funny, not so long ago I was happy over a doughnut. Now, I was in a bed getting served breakfast. Maybe my life had changed.

"So, how did it go? Was it everything you imagined? I bet they were fantastic." Pat grabbed a strawberry.

"It was perfect. So, where are they? I thought one of them was supposed to keep guard." I waved at the chair. "Even yesterday when they had their meeting they had Jamal stand outside my door."

"They are getting ready to go get the bag." Pat looked at me as if this was common knowledge.

I jumped out of bed. Not without me they aren't. They would never know which brick to look behind. It was bad enough for them going down there.

They were Elite's. If they started snooping someone could get the wrong idea and attack them. It was one thing to go asking for a service, it was another to dig through things. It was way too dangerous.

Pat called out to me as I ran down the hall. Ignoring him I went right to Aiden's office. I flung open the door. Nothing. Shit, where did they go?

Running down the hall I grabbed the nearest servant, "Where are The Trips?"

"Preparing to leave. I believe they are already in their car," he answered.

"Thanks," I called out as I ran.

"Ma'am, you are just in a t-shirt," he called out to me.

I didn't give a damn.

My men were in their fancy black car halfway down the driveway. I chased after them. The tires came to a screeching halt, forcing the car to slightly fishtail. They were out of the car and on me faster than I could open my mouth.

Derek had one arm, Jason had the other, and Aiden was standing in front of me. I could have been wrong but I was pretty sure smoke was coming from their ears. To say they looked pissed would be an understatement. They shouldn't have been pissed, I was. They were leaving without me.

"Are you fucking kidding me?" Aiden roared.

"Me? You were about to leave!" I pointed to the car.

"That gives you a right to come outside in that?" Aiden grabbed my t-shirt. "We weren't clear?"

"What?" I asked.

"You are ours!" Derek growled in my ear.

"Oh my, you guys are being ridiculous." I pushed Aiden. "I'm covered! You can't see anything."

His finger was under the t-shirt and inside my pussy before I blinked. I bit my lip. Fuck, he was so good with his fingers. I clenched around his touch.

As quickly as he did it his finger was gone. I squeezed my legs.

"I don't need to see!" Aiden took his finger and licked my juices from it. "I can feel!"

"So? I ran out here to make sure you guys didn't leave without me. It's not like people are gonna stop and finger me!" I snapped.

"Keep it up and all three of us will have our fingers up in you," Derek laughed. It wasn't his normal ha ha, it was more sinister and laced with anger.

I looked to Jason aside from grabbing my arm he hadn't said anything. Not that he said much, but I expected something from him.

"No, don't give me those puppy dog eyes. You fucked up." Jason gripped my arm tighter.

Okay, so all three of them were pissed at me. It wasn't like I was naked running around. Plus, we hadn't established rules about attire. Not that I would listen, they weren't gonna dictate what I wore. Yes, I was gonna go inside and put clothes on, but that wasn't the point.

"Point made. Now, will you three wait while I go get dressed. You can't go without me." I attempted to give them all puppy dog eyes. "It's dangerous."

"Actually, I don't think our point is made." Derek looked to Aiden and Jason. "Do you guys?"

They both shook their heads.

Jason and Derek guided me over to the car. Derek rubbed my bare ass. Tingles ran up my spine. My heartbeat quickened. They were gonna punish me. My pussy dripped.

Aiden bent me over the car. Derek continued to rub my ass. I could have fought back. Reminded them we were out in the open. Honestly I was too excited about what they were about to do to me to say anything.

"I think you need to be punished," Aiden growled in my ear.

"For wearing a t-shirt?" I was purposely being a brat.

"For not covering up what's ours." Jason grabbed my hair, pulled my face to his and kissed me.

I rubbed my legs together.

Derek lifted my shirt exposing my ass.

Aiden rubbed my ass then slapped it. The sting excited me. He did it again, slightly harder this time. My pussy dripped. I wanted more.

Jason took Aiden's place and spanked me. He bent down and kissed the spot he hit. Then spanked me again.

Derek got behind me. The thought of him also hitting my ass sent my skin on fire. His dick slid between my cheeks rubbing against my pussy. Oh shit. He was gonna fuck me out in the open on his car.

His cock entered me. He wasn't gentle. While he rammed his cock in and out of me the other two slapped my ass. This was the best punishment ever.

"Who do you belong to?" Aiden grabbed my face.

"Uhhh,,," I couldn't speak. I was getting so close to the edge.

"Answer!" Aiden demanded.

"Y...Yo...Ahhh Fuck...You." Vibrations ran through my veins.

"Just Aiden?" Derek rammed his cock in harder, deeper.

Jason reached his hand down and rubbed my clit. Fuck, my body was on fire. I grabbed Aiden. My body shook.

"Naughty Girl, answer or we stop." Jason rubbed my clit up and down slowly bringing me so close to the edge while his brother fucked me.

"No. A...All of you g...guys. Shit." I was coming hard. "I belong to all three of you!" I screamed as the vibrations took over my body.

Derek pulled out and pressed his dick against my leg. The wetness dripped down. He came down my leg marking what was his. I had never tasted cum. Getting the sudden urge, I reached my hand down and touched where he came. I licked his cum from my finger, tasting the salty sweetness. Damn, I enjoyed it.

"Fuck, did you really just?" Aiden grabbed me and kissed my forehead. "Forgiven."

"Shit, you are forgiven. That was hot." Derek grabbed my shirt and pulled it down.

"You are gonna have to taste all of us soon." Jason licked his finger that was on my clit. "But we have to go."

"Not without me." I crossed my arms.

"We can handle ourselves. You need to stay here where it's

safe." Aiden pointed to the house.

"I'm going to pretend you didn't forget that I grew up there and was part of the dangers of the streets." I shook my head. "You don't get it. Elite's and Rich go there for services. You three start poking around and searching behind dumpsters and they will attack you."

"Awe, Babe, don't worry we got big muscles." Derek winked.

"Please," I begged.

Twenty minutes later I was showered, dressed and in the car with them, heading to my old neighborhood. Ha, how quickly I considered The Trips home my own. It was like the second they claimed me they put a spell on me. I was theirs and they were mine. Which meant their home was now mine. Along with the beautiful library that I planned on taking full advantage of, well when I wasn't with them.

It didn't take us long to get to my old alley. Nothing had changed. I didn't know why I expected it to be different, but I did. Without Vickie and I here, I had thought maybe the atmosphere would be heavier, sadder, lonely. Yet, it was the exact same.

People walked around and did the same thing they always did. They were all in the same spots I had left them in. Some whispered in corners, others slept by their dumpsters. A few tried to sell to us as we walked by. Did they not recognize me? I looked down. I was wearing tight jeans, brand new sneakers and had freshly combed hair. Yea, I wouldn't have recognized me either.

When we reached my old dumpster, a younger woman was sitting on my milk crates picking at her nails. It was the same woman that had ratted me out to The Trips. She must have moved into my spot the second I left.

"Excuse me Ma'am. We need you to move for a few minutes." Aiden looked down at her.

"Fuck off. This is my spot." She continued to pick at her nails.

"Actually, that's my spot!" I snapped. She couldn't just steal my spot!

"You think I'm gonna believe an Elite owns a place down here." She waved her hand at me. "Don't you guys own enough?"

I grabbed her by the throat and shoved her against the brick wall. She blinked fast but kept her eyes on me. "Look you little priss. I'm Kira. Kira the finder. Ever heard of me?"

She nodded.

"Good. Now my boyfriend asked you to move. I suggest you listen." I released her throat.

"Correction. Boyfriends. We all wanted her to move." Derek waved his hand at himself and Jason.

My heart flipped. I hadn't realized what I said until he pointed it out and corrected me. Boyfriends! Fuck, I was lucky.

"Kira the finder would never be caught dead with Elite's." The woman crossed her arms over her chest.

"Don't talk to me like you know anything about what I would do. You ratted me out to these guys a few weeks ago. Now move." I went to go for her throat again, but she got up.

Jason and Derek moved the dumpster aside.

An older gentleman with three others came strolling down the alley. We didn't have leaders. Just people who looked out for others. Old Man was one of those people. Old Man had been in his share of fights and had the scars to prove it. He didn't take too kindly to someone taking advantage of another homeless person.

"Excuse me, what are you doing?" Old Man asked.

"Hey, Old Man. Sorry, I just had to get something." I

smiled.

He tossed his arms around me. My men growled. I lifted a hand up to let them know I was alright.

"Kira? You look...look. Well you look like them." Old Man jabbed a thumb toward The Trips.

"Long story. We are just getting something and this woman can go back to my spot." I glared at the woman.

"Of course." he gave a head nod and the people with him walked away. He gave me another quick hug and joined them.

As soon as he was gone I removed the brick behind the dumpster.

Fuck.

Nothing.

It was empty.

No one knew of my hiding place. Not even Vickie.

Fuck.

"Guys we have a problem," I whispered.

"What?" Aiden asked calmly, but the anger was evident.

"It's gone." I dropped the brick.

"Did anyone come here? Snoop around?" I grabbed the woman by the shirt and slammed her against the wall.

She nodded.

"Who?" my voice shook. Shit, my whole body was shaking.

"Another of you people," she whispered. "The guy who you were talking to before. Um, before they came to get you."

I dropped her and turned to the men. "I know who has the bag."

"And?" they all asked simultaneously.

"The man who paid me to steal it. A man named Carlos Garcia." I clenched my fists.

"He paid you? Are you fucking kidding me, Kira?" Aiden growled.

"You know him?" I scrunched up my face.

CHAPTER 18

## *Kira and the dress*

Twenty-four hours later and my mind was still racing. The Triplets had meetings with their Grandfather so they asked me to stay in my room. Since I had so many books there I agreed. The problem was I couldn't read. I couldn't do anything, but try to connect the dots on what happened.

Carlos Garcia was after the same property as The Trips. Apparently he was a bottom of the barrel Elite. He was practically Rich as Derek explained. He had been trying to grow his status and couldn't get ahead. The Trips had no intention of trampling his dream. The property they wanted served a much bigger purpose and they were going to own it. Of course they wouldn't tell me the purpose.

Jason believed Carlos paid me to steal from them to use the contents of the bag as leverage. He said what was in the bag was enough to make them back out of the property. If that was the only way to get it back, they would step down and allow Carlos to buy it.

Shit, that was all my fault. Had I not stolen it they wouldn't have been in that position. I tried to ask them why the bag was so important. All I got from them was it was one of Jason's inventions. That dude was seriously smart.

I got out of the shower and tossed on some shorts and a tank top. According to Pat he would be back soon with a few of the servants. They were dressing me for the party tonight. I had never been to a party. I crashed a few to steal things, but I never got to enjoy them. Tonight I would not only be invited, but I was with the men throwing the party.

What did someone wear to a fancy ass party? I would soon find out. I had assumed it would be some over the top big fluffy, hard to walk in dresses and suits for the men. Yea, in my head they all dressed like Aiden. I couldn't wait to see all three of my men dressed up. Hopefully after the party they would come by and rip my dress off of me.

The door flew open and Pat sauntered in with an entourage. Five women came in carrying dresses and suitcases. How much stuff did he think I needed? My mouth fell open. The women busied themselves around the room setting up. One of them even put together a rack to put the dresses on.

Thankfully none of the dresses were what I expected. They were all sleek and elegant. I didn't even own a dress and now I was about to try on a bunch. I smiled as I skimmed the rack.

"Aren't they all just darling?" Pat clasped his hands together. "I picked every one out just for you. Now, there is one small thing. Once you pick one out it has to go to The Trips for a final approval. Oh, but don't worry it'll be back in enough time for the big night.

"I can't believe I get to try these on." A black silk one slid through my fingers. I ignored what he said about 'final approval,' they couldn't dictate what I wore.

"Sweetie, you are gonna look gorgeous." He grabbed a red one with a low cut front and handed it to me. "Now try this on while the girls set up hair and make-up."

"Huh?" My eyes bugged out of my head.

"You are The Trips' special guest, so yes you get the works." Pat waved me to the bathroom.

As I was trying on the dress my stomach dropped. Yes, this was all perfect, but something was off. I would be getting all glammed up while Vickie served me my drinks? It wasn't right. She deserved this way more than I did.

I stepped out of the bathroom in my shorts. There was no way I could do this. I would tell Pat I had to speak to The Trips and get this straightened out.

"Sweetie, did it not fit?" He pursed his lips.

"It's not that...it's," I started to explain.

"So sorry I'm late." The door flew open and hit the wall. Vickie stood in the entrance catching her breath.

"Vickie!" I ran over and threw my arms around her. "I'm so happy you are here. I have to tell The Trips if you aren't invited as a guest to this party then I'm not going."

"Why do you think I'm here?" she asked. "They wanted me to go. They are even letting Miguel go. You and I are getting ready together."

My heart sped fast. They did this for me. They knew I would want her there. Fuck, they really were perfect. "Tell me all about Miguel."

"He's wonderful. I met him in the backyard. He does the cool bushes. He used to paint on the streets until Pat found him. He brought him here and got him a job. The Trips said if he is as good as he says, they are gonna have him paint murals for them. How cool." Vickie scanned the dresses looking for one that might fit her tiny frame.

"You two have plenty of time to talk of love." Pat clapped his hands. "Let's go."

I went back into the bathroom and put the red dress on. Vickie grabbed a dress in a much smaller size and put it on. It was silver and truly made her look like a fairy. It was perfect.

As for the red dress, I hated it. The thing had two large slits up the front that went past my hips. One wrong move and my vagina would fall out. Nope. The Trips would never approve, not that I cared. Okay, maybe I did. I wanted them to be stunned, not pissed.

Pat handed me three more dresses that were equally as revealing in their own way.

"Is there something here that doesn't scream I can afford fabric but chose not to?" I asked him after the fourth dress was so low cut it showed my belly button. I'm not knocking someone else's fashion choices, but on me I didn't like it and I knew my men would hate them.

"Last one before we have to consider some alterations." He handed me the black silky dress.

It slid over my skin as if it belonged there. It had thin straps, and fell down to the floor in pools around my ankles. There were no slits or boob malfunctions. It was perfect. I walked out of the bathroom to show them.

Everyone gasped. I blushed. Vickie nodded relentlessly. She still hadn't taken off the silver one. Neither one of us had ever worn something so expensive. So perfect.

Pat clapped his hand and then pulled out a pair of shoes from one of the suitcases. "These will be perfect."

They were black strappy things with heels the size of nails. Ha. he couldn't possibly think I was gonna wear those. I wouldn't be able to walk three feet in those, yet alone wear them during an entire party. "I can't wear those."

"Sweetie, they would be perfect." He stared at me. "Okay fine. I have a pair of boring flats. Luckily with the dress and mask no one will be looking at your feet."

"Mask?" Vickie and I asked simultaneously.

"Didn't they tell you? It's a masquerade ball. It's their grandfather's favorite kind of party." Pat pulled out multiple masks.

They were all colorful with feathers and glitter. All of them were beautiful. Pat handed Vickie a silver one with pink feathers. It made her look even more the fairy than she already was.

He sorted through all the masks and set them aside. I reached my hand out to touch one and he swatted it away. Finally at the bottom of the suitcase he pulled one out and handed it to me. It was all black without feathers or glitter. It was simple yet made a huge statement. It was in the shape of a wolf.

"The boys have requested you wear this one." Pat tied the ribbon behind me so I could try it on.

"It's beautiful," I smiled.

"A ball," Vickie whispered. "Can you believe we are going to a ball?"

I had thought getting ready would be quick and easy. Boy was I wrong. Hair alone took hours. The ladies fussed over it until they said it was perfect. It was in a side braid with pieces cascading down framing my face. As if that wasn't enough, they added jewels into the braid. Then make-up took even longer. I didn't understand it, but Vickie seemed to be really enjoying all of it.

A few minutes before the party started and we were finally ready to go. Miguel showed up at my door to pick up Vickie and escort her into the party. He was in a tux with a silver bowtie to match Vickie. They looked adorable and the smile on her face was genuine.

As soon as they walked away The Trips showed up at my door. All three of them had on tuxes and matching shiny shoes. I laughed, they were identical. I mean there was no way I could tell them apart. At all. To top it off they all had on black wolf masks that matched mine. We were a pack and it was perfect.

"Shit Babe, I could just eat you up." Derek wrapped me up in a hug and kissed me. "Which I will do later."

"Stunning." Jason held out a single rose for me and then kissed me.

"Did you know your dress comes with pockets?" Aiden grinned.

"No, so cool." I shoved my hands in the pockets. "Fuck they have holes in the bottom. I can't put anything in them."

Aiden slid his hand in my pocket. His fingertips grazed my skin. "No, but we can touch you whenever we want." He brought his hand close to my pussy and rubbed the fabric of my underwear.

Fuck. They put holes in my pockets so they could finger me in a room full of people. I was instantly wet.

Aiden removed his hand and then kissed me. "Ready?"

I nodded.

One of the rooms that was normally emptied now housed the ball. It, like everything in the mansion, was massive. String lights hung from the ceiling and ran along the walls. Tall tables were placed in clusters in various spots. A bar was set up in the corner. Tables among tables held more food than I had ever seen in one place. My stomach rumbled, reminding me that hair and makeup got in the way of eating.

When we entered, the room fell silent. So many people were there and I just walked in with the hosts. I wanted to be invisible. Every eye was on me. I hated it. I wanted to melt right into the floor and disappear.

"My grandsons and their beautiful date, Kira Jones." Their Grandfather waved in our direction.

Everyone held up a glass to us. The heat burning in my face was enough to put the sun to shame. The Trips did a quick nod and everyone took a sip from their glass.

"Can I leave now?" I whispered to Aiden.

"Stop it. This is gonna be fun." Derek tossed his arm around me.

Jason grabbed me and pulled me onto the dance floor. I had no clue what I was doing, but he took the lead. He twirled me around and then pulled me in close. It was a slower song so I got the hang of the beat quickly.

After we were done Derek cut in and pulled me over to the food table. Everything was delicious. There were little shrimps, cucumbers with cheese, and little sandwiches. It was amazing. I gulped down champagne and ate more than my share of food.

Aiden slipped in behind me and put his hand in my pocket. His finger pushed my panties to the side. He rubbed my clit. I gasped.

People were all around. Many nodded at Aiden as they passed us. None of them knew what he was doing to me. My breathing hastened. I bit my lip drawing blood. He rubbed harder.

I came on his finger. My balance swayed. His other hand steadied me. Jason walked over and handed me another glass of champagne. I gulped it down in one sip.

Attempting to catch my breath I watched the people. All of them clueless as to how lucky they were. None of them had ever wondered where their next meal came from or where they were going to sleep. Their lives were perfect. Mr. Cartright stood in the center laughing with others and the most oblivious of all of them. He had everything.

He must have noticed me because he made a b-line toward us and stopped at me. He grabbed my hand and gave it a quick kiss. Shit, no one taught me what the fuck I was supposed to do. So I stood there unblinking and motionless.

"They told me they found a woman, but didn't mention exactly how gorgeous you are." He dropped my hand.

"Um, thank you, Sir." I blinked repeatedly. Shit, I had to get my shit together.

"May I have this dance?" He pointed to a dance floor where a few people were dancing in circles.

"Oh, I can't." I shook my head.

"I know they dance in Tentokesee." He grabbed my hand. "I insist."

He pulled me to the dance floor. I tried to stop him and couldn't. This was going to go badly. It was different with Jason, we just twirled in circles. He placed one hand on the small of my back and the other grabbed my free hand. I stepped on his foot.

"Oh come on, I would think a thief would have better balance," he whispered.

My stomach twisted.

"My grandsons aren't the only ones with workers in these walls." He twirled me around.

I fumbled and was about to fall on my face when he grabbed me and pulled me into him.

"Um..um..I'm no thi..thief," I stammered. I had to get out of here. Pat had said he was worried about the family. If they put me on trial I would be dead.

"Let's not lie to each other. Look, I don't care about what you are. My issue is with what you stole," he whispered in my ear.

"I tried to get it back," I snapped. Shit, I just admitted it.

"It's funny. Had you known what you stole, I'm sure you wouldn't have," he chuckled. "Instead, you, a homeless, stole a weapon against the homeless and gave it to the one person who wants to use it against your kind." He twirled me again. This time I kept my balance.

"Weapon?" My throat ran dry.

"It's a GPS tracking device for humans. Jason created it for the military. No more prisoners of war. The Government decided it was too inhumane. The Elites wanted to use it to keep track of the homeless. Imagine a life where you had to be permitted to go anywhere. Unless you had a work visa you couldn't leave your street. That's what Carlos wants." He kept dancing like he wasn't dropping bombs on me.

"The Government? They don't exist anymore." My heart slammed into my chest. I thought it would break a rib.

"Oh they exist, just not to your kind. Who do you think controls the military? The Government had decided to abandon the homeless. Too much of a waste of money." He grinned.

"Wait, Jason said Carlos wanted it for leverage. Not to track the homeless." The room was too heavy, the air too hot. My ears pounded.

"Jason may not know. They think the Nant-bots are useless without the codes. They don't know Carlos had been working on a reprogramming code that would also allow it to be self destructive. That means when a homeless person is out of bounds their brains get splattered."

"Why would Carlos care about the homeless?" I asked.

"Rumor has it he had an issue with a maid a while back. Now he is out for revenge on the homeless." He shrugged.

"So why are you telling me all this?" I tried to keep my thoughts straight. This information was priceless. Not to mention it didn't sound like his own grandsons knew everything, well almost everything.

"I asked about you. Kira the finder. You are the best. I wanna make a deal." He stopped dancing and looked me in the eyes.

I nodded.

"Steal the bag from Carlos and I won't slice you from ear to ear." He grabbed my face.

"Why do you give a fuck if Carlos controls homeless?" I tried to steady my voice.

"I don't. My grandsons do. It's their weakness. Not surprised they fell in love with one. I am about to turn over everything I have built to them. I don't need them distracted."

"So what do I get if I do get the bag?" I stared him in the eyes.

"Aside from living?" He scratched his face. "You don't seem to care so much about your own life. Okay, how about if you don't, I will take everything from my grandsons and leave them homeless. Because if you don't get that bag back they will lose everything trying to get it back. They would give up everything to protect your kind."

"How do you know that? They could just shrug it off." Yes, I cared deeply for The Trips but I doubted they would give up everything to stop the homeless from getting trackers in them.

"Trust me." He pulled me into a hug. "Now go before I slice you in front of them."

## CHAPTER 19

## Kira and the distraction

I WASN'T SCARED OF HIM. SHIT, HIS OWN GRANDSONS had threatened me on multiple occasions. That wasn't why I couldn't breathe. No, it was fear for my men. I believed this man would take everything from them. I also believed he would kill me in front of them. That was something I didn't want them to see. No matter what that man thought of me, I cared for my own life. Self preservation had kept me alive this long.

Without another word I headed to the bathroom. When no one was paying attention to me I would be gone. Derek grabbed me around the waist before I reached the door. I hadn't realized how hard it was to be invisible with three boyfriends.

"Hey Babe." Derek slid his hand into my pocket and grazed my skin.

"Oh, hi. Um, I gotta head to the bathroom." I pulled away from him.

"You okay?" He searched my face.

"Yea. Could you grab Vickie for me?" I hugged him and

slid my hand in his pocket grabbing his keys without him noticing. "I got um, female issues."

Derek nodded and took off.

Vickie was in the bathroom with me within minutes. She pulled tampons and pads from her purse. A condom fell out as she was searching. The girl was always prepared.

"No, I'm good. I need help." I paced.

"Oh Derek said female stuff. So I thought." She put the products back in her purse. "So what's up?"

"I have to sneak out of here." I pulled up my dress to my knees and knotted it. "Not just the party. I mean the mansion."

"Why? I thought." Vickie wiped a tear from her cheek. "We have everything here. Don't you love The Trips? I just..."

I grabbed Vickie's shoulders and shook her. "Stop it. I'll be back. I just have to do something. Please help. I need a distraction."

Vickie batted away more tears. "Not unless you tell me what you're up to and I mean everything."

"Okay, but you can't tell anyone. Not even Miguel." I paced.

She nodded.

"Their grandfather threatened to take everything from them and kill me unless I steal back the bag I stole in the first place. The person who paid me, Carlos Garcia will use the stuff against The Trips unless I get it back. Their Grandfather wants to ensure no one has anything against his grandsons. That's the gist of it anyway." I grabbed her bag and looked through it for any weapons.

She had a metal nail file which I placed in my bra. I also took a pen and put it in the elastic of my underwear. At least the holes in the pockets would make it easy to grab.

"Do you have to do this tonight?" she asked.

"Yes, now will you help?" I grabbed her hands. "I need a distraction."

"Okay, I'll do it." She pulled me in for a hug. "You better be safe."

Vickie left the bathroom. I waited for whatever distraction she was going to pull. Rubbing my hands together I thought of my next move. I wasn't sure how I was going to break into the house and get the bag back without any intel. I didn't know where he was hiding it or how to get it. I liked robbing people in the middle of the day, not at night. Mr. Cartright didn't seem like a patient person. There would be no time to set up a proper heist.

"Help!" someone screamed.

Perfect. I slipped from the bathroom and down the hall. Everyone was at the party. The few servants that were in the hall were running toward the commotion. I didn't know what she did, but it worked. No one paid attention to me.

I walked right out the front door. The security that was outside was running inside to help. I hopped in The Triplets black car and used the keys I took from Derek. Driving wasn't my strong suit.

Swerving, I left the driveway and hit a few bushes along the way. After a few minutes I got a little better at it. Luckily not too many people drove in New Boston so the streets were empty. Anytime I saw a person walking I slowed down to a crawl so I wouldn't swerve and hit them.

I managed to get to Guy's place rather quickly. His shop was closed up but I knew he slept in the back. Banging on the door, I shouted until he unlocked it. He was wearing boxers and nothing else. His gut hung lower than his waistband and his greasy hair framed his face.

"Come on, Kira. Shop is closed." Guy took a drag from his cigarette.

"I need some knives and some nanos." I pushed past him into his shop.

"No." Guy slammed his door and followed me inside.

"I wasn't asking." I walked into his storage room on the right. It was where he held the expensive stuff. His everyday items were in the front so people could peruse them.

"I heard the rumors. You are living with The Cartrights." He took another drag from his cigarette and blew it in my direction. "Shit, look at you. You look Elite. I'm not helping you."

I pulled the box with the knives down and set them on a nearby table.

Guy grabbed my arm and twisted me to him. I reached into my pocket and took out the pen. It was against his throat before he could blink. There was no time for his games. "Like I said, I wasn't asking."

"Fine. Take what you want Kira. Just pay me back. Okay?" Guy took a step back.

I turned back to the box and took out a few of the smaller knives. Violence wasn't my thing. Being invisible was the best way to get around. The problem was sometimes, I didn't have that luxury. Since there wasn't much time to steal from Carlos, I had to be prepared.

After I strapped a few knives to my legs and one to my arm I filled a tin with some nano's and took one of the pens that controlled them.

Guy didn't say another word to me as I left. He knew he would get his money so I didn't know why he was being such an ass. Oh well.

Once I left his shop I headed right for Garcia Corp. I had plan A and Plan B. Until I got there I wasn't sure which one I was going to go with. Plan A required me sneaking in and convincing a servant to tell me where the bag was. Hopefully they would know where it was or at least where Carlos kept his precious cargo. Plan B was to find Carlos and hold a knife to his throat until he told me where it was. Neither plan was that great but that was all I had.

When I pulled up to the complex I realized neither of those plans would work. Every light was on in the building and outside. Anyone working there just saw me pull in. There would be no sneaking in. Looks like I was taking the full on walk in approach.

I unstrapped the knife from my arm and untied the knot in my dress. After ruffling my hair, I pulled up closer. A man in a blue uniform stepped up to the car.

Stumbling out of the car I leaned into him. He grabbed me and steadied me.

"Sir, I'm so sorry." I fanned myself. "I may have drank too much."

"It's okay Ma'am. I got you." He wrapped his arm around me and led me inside.

The inside was in full motion. People were walking around and working like it wasn't late at night. A man was even washing the windows. It was late. Did they ever stop?

"Why is everyone still working?" I stumbled, trying to act as drunk as possible.

"Mr. Garcia doesn't believe in breaks." He brought me over to a chair and sat me down. "Would you like a glass of water?"

"Yes, please." I nodded. "It seems harsh to have no breaks."

"All Elite are like that." He covered his mouth and mumbled. "Sorry I mean no disrespect, I enjoy all the work."

"Oh no. It's fine." I fanned myself. "Is there a bathroom around here?"

Maybe my plan would still work if I could get one of the servants one on one. Not this guy. He was too businesslike. He probably enjoyed working for Carlos.

A clapping started at the top of the stairs across from me.

Everyone stopped. The man I had met in the alley was skipping down the steps. He continued clapping as he reached the bottom of the stairs. There was something in the way he smiled that made my skin crawl.

I stood to get up. The man in the blue uniform placed his hand on my shoulder and pushed me back down. Fuck.

"Kira the finder." Carlos walked toward me. "Welcome."

"How?" It was all I could think of to say.

"Mr. Cartright," he smiled.

"Why?" Words weren't coming easily to me.

"I made a deal with him. You in exchange for the Nantbots. Between me and you, he isn't getting them. I have my best guys working on reprogramming them." He nodded to the man in blue.

The man grabbed me and pulled me upright. I yanked my arm to get away. Metal clinked against my wrists. Handcuffs. I took a deep breath. I was so fucked.

"You are double crossing them?" I pulled against the cuffs like it was gonna do something.

"Hey, I get everything. I'll be a hero to the rest of The Elite. They can't stand homeless. Plus there is you. I get to have you." Carlos pulled up a chair and sat down.

The man in blue pushed me down into the chair across from him.

"Let me tell you a story. A few years ago, I fell in love. She was perfect. She was beautiful, smart, and funny. There was one problem, she was a homeless. I know right. Me. Fall in love with your kind. Silly, right?" He sat back in the chair and laughed. "I knew she loved me too. She even said so."

"What does that have to do with anything?" I snapped.

"Be patient. So anyway. I asked her to run away with me. She refused. Said she couldn't leave her precious daughter on the streets. I didn't mean to hurt her." He put his face in his hands. "I loved her. I didn't mean to get so angry with her.

"I was heartbroken. A part of me was missing. Then a few weeks ago I heard your name. Kira the finder. I knew it had to be you. That day I had only meant to see you. I just wanted to see your face. Then I realized, I could have everything I wanted. The bots and her back."

My stomach turned. Sweat poured down my temples. I squeezed my eyes shut to stop the tears. I didn't want to believe what he was saying. Maybe I was wrong. Maybe he wasn't talking about her.

"Don't you see. You were the reason she wouldn't leave with me. How could a mother leave her daughter? Once I saw you, I got it. You are a spitting image of your mother.

I needed you but I couldn't grab you off the streets. The homeless riff raff would have torn me to pieces. I had to get you to my house. So I paid you to steal from the Cartrights. Two birds, one stone. I couldn't believe you got caught. I had to have you. Then Mr. Cartright asked what it would take to get the Nant-bots back. So, I told him you. Not that he is getting the bots back. Now I have everything. To think, he managed to get you to walk in." Carlos cupped my face with his hand.

I leaned up and slammed my face into his. Blood poured. A gash was across his forehead. I went in to head butt him again. The man in the blue uniform grabbed me. My stomach turned.

The Trips would never find me. Even if they did, Carlos would never let them get to me. How long before they realized I was gone? Too long. Maybe if Carlos kept me here they would find me. If they did, would Carlos hurt them, or kill them?

"Get her up. We are leaving, her men will never find her." Carlos said to the man in blue.

I pulled against the man. They would never find me. Fuck. Tears streamed down my face. I finally found the men I was supposed to spend the rest of my life with. I loved them. Now I would never see them again. I spit at Carlos.

"You are feisty." Carlos wiped his forehead. "I'll tame that right out of you."

CHAPTER 20

## *Aiden and the mini globe*

WATCHING MY GRANDFATHER DANCE WITH HER
turned my stomach. It was in the way he looked at her. His
eyes sparkled as if she was a piece of meat. I wanted to step in.
The only people that should have been that close to her were
my brothers and me. That was it. I didn't trust my grandfather. Never did.

He twirled her around. She was pale and looked scared.
Fuck. He said something vile to her. That man was a snake. I
walked toward them.

"What a lovely party." Miss Baker stepped in my path.

"Thank you." I stepped out of the way.

"You boys are always great at throwing parties." She
stepped back in my way and put her hand on my chest. Miss
Baker was widowed years ago and rumor had it she was
looking for someone to marry.

"Thank you. Now, if you'll excuse me." I grabbed her by
the shoulders and pushed her to the side.

Kira was gone. My grandfather had turned to someone else
and was chatting it up with them. I looked around for her and

didn't see her anywhere. Derek came over to me with a smile on his face. How was he always so happy?

"Have you seen Kira?" Derek asked. "I wanted to stick my hands in her pockets."

"No. Check the bathroom." I slapped him on the back. Once he was done I would get my chance to play with her, again. My dick grew from the thought of it.

My Grandfather was still talking to someone when I reached him. I interrupted the conversation and pulled him to the side. "What did you say to Kira?"

"Lovely girl. I can see why you three want her." He took a sip of his drink.

"She looked upset. What did you say to her?" I clenched my fists.

"Would you relax? I didn't say anything to her. Maybe she wasn't feeling well." He patted my shoulder. "You could take a page from Derek's book. Even Jason isn't so uptight."

A table crashed. I turned. Vickie was standing by the now fallen dessert table holding her throat. Her face was a beat red. She started slapping her chest.

"Help!" Miss Baker screamed. She was slapping Vickie's back.

Everyone ran over to her. Vickie fell to the ground. Miguel was on her, blocking my view. Others tried to push him aside, but he wouldn't budge.

The air was wrong. My stomach was heavy. Something was off. Where was Kira? There was no way her friend was lying on the ground choking and she wasn't there. It wasn't in her nature to not help someone she loved. Hell, we had used her love for Vickie against her.

Pat was standing above Vickie crying and begging someone to help. I stomped over to him and grabbed him by the arm. He protested at first, until he saw it was me. Dragging him to my office, I didn't say a word.

"Boss, are you okay?" he asked the second the door shut.

"Without alerting anyone, you are going to find Kira!" I ground my teeth.

"Huh? She was at the party. I can go get her." Pat pointed to the door.

"Something is up. Once Vickie stops with her pretend choking act you are to get her alone and find out where Kira is." My Grandfather had to have scared her. Maybe he told her to leave. Maybe he threatened her with something. Either way this was the quickest way to get information. Vickie would be more inclined to tell Pat than me.

Pat nodded and speed walked out of the office. While he was gone I paced. I wanted to believe Kira didn't take off. Maybe she had just gotten sick and went to her room. Maybe she had too much caviar and was in the bathroom getting sick. I didn't believe those things. My gut told me something happened with my grandfather,

It didn't take long before Pat returned. I had been inspecting my mini globe when he sauntered back in. He was holding his chest and breathing heavy.

"Boss, Vickie said. Um. She said...well." Pat fanned himself. "Kira went to get the bag back."

"She did what?!" I tossed the mini globe I had been holding against the wall.

Pat backed away and averted his eyes. "She went to...um... get it back."

I grabbed my keys off the desk and stormed out of the office.

"Where ar-are yo-you going?" Pat stammered.

"I'm going to get my brothers and we are getting our woman back."

"Boss, you can't. It'll start a war," Pat pleaded.

"Do you think I give a fuck about a war? She's all that matters!" I slammed the door.

Fuck! Why would she do that? Carlos had security every-where. She wouldn't get within a mile of that place. He would have her killed. Then we would kill him. A war? Who gave a damn. We would crush him.

Derek and Jason were walking toward me in the hall. Both had scowls on their faces. They knew something was up.

"She went to get the bag back," I growled the second they were in earshot.

"We are gonna need weapons," Derek grinned. "I have some in my room."

"Why? You know what. Never mind." Jason shook his head.

We headed to Derek's room and grabbed some knives he had. Jason took off to his room to grab some bots that spit acid. That dude was a genius. He turned nanos and small robots into anything he imagined. It was part of why we were in this mess, but it also brought Kira to us, so who was I to complain.

When we got outside all three of us cursed. Our main car was gone. Kira. She took it which meant she was ahead of us by a lot. She could already be there. If Carlos touched her he would be dead.

We ran to the garage to grab a different car. The jeep would work. None of us said anything as we jumped in and sped off to Carlos Corp. He lived at his corporation. If she knew that then she would be there.

All the lights were on. Was he having a party? No. Most couldn't stand him. He had to pay workers just to have company.

No one stopped us from walking right in. Servants walked around busying themselves. None of them said anything to us. Jason grabbed my arm before I took another step. Carlos' voice.

"Don't you see. You were the reason she wouldn't leave

with me. How could a mother leave her daughter? Once I saw you, I got it. You are a spitting image of your mother.

I needed you but I couldn't grab you off the streets." Carlo's voice boomed off the walls.

That fucking piece of shit. He thought he could steal our woman. Our footsteps quickened. Carlos kept talking but I couldn't hear. Either his voice grew too low or the blood in my veins rushed too loudly.

We ran.

Carlos was in a chair across from Kira. Blood poured from his head. I couldn't see Kira's face. I didn't know if she was hurt. A man held her in the chair.

She lunged forward, Screaming. Carlos backed up and fell backward in the chair. That was our girl. The man that was holding her grabbed her by the hair. She was yanked backward forcefully.

Derek reached him first. The knife in his hand sliced into the man's neck as if it was a tender steak. Blood poured. I smiled.

"Are you insane!" Carlos screamed, clamoring from the chair.

Jason grabbed him from behind and pressed a knife to his throat. Then he let out a low whistle. A hundred tiny bots crawled up Carlos' legs. He tried to kick them away but Jason whispered something in his ear which stopped him.

"Baby, are you okay?" I asked Kira, pulling her into me.

Footsteps echoed. A dozen guards showed up. A little late if you asked me, but they weren't my security.

"Take one step and he dies." Jason turned Carlos so they could see.

"You came." She rested her head on my chest.

"Of course. You are ours." I kissed the top of her head. "Are you okay?"

"I'm okay. I need to be uncuffed so I can kill this fucker." She spat in Carlos' direction.

"We got this." I kissed the top of her head.

She pulled away from me. "He killed my mother. I'm going to kill him." Tears streamed down her face.

"Fuck off, Bitch." Carlos mumbled.

"I wouldn't speak to her like that." Derek wiped the knife covered in blood on his pant leg. "That'll get you killed faster."

"You guys are really gonna kill me over a homeless? That isn't how Elite's handle disputes," Carlos scoffed. The way he said homeless boiled my blood. He had no right. "If you want the bots, take them. They are in my office."

"We will deal with the backlash." Jason pressed the knife deeper against his throat. Blood trickled down. "The bots are the least of our concern."

I looked at Kira. Her eyes were big and pleading. She wanted to be the one to kill him. She needed to be. After this I would have to ask her how her mother was killed by this man. Now wasn't the time.

How could I deny her?

Derek had sensed the same thing he was searching through the dead man's pockets. He pulled out the keys and tossed them to me.

I turned to the security guards and staff. "Carlos has a sister Maria. He banished her years ago to Peru. In the morning I will send for her. She will be your new boss. I trust no one has an issue with this."

While Carlos was busy trying to buy out properties we wanted, I was busy getting information on his family. Most of them were dead. One mysterious accident after another. All except his sister.

I had talked to her on the phone once. She said as long as he lived, she wouldn't step foot in New Boston. Well that problem was about to be solved. I just hoped she was a better person than Carlos.

The security guards all put up their hands and stepped away.

"You guys are all dead!" Carlos screamed. "You can't get away with this."

He struggled against the knife. A bot spit acid at him. He screamed. Blood trickled from his neck.

Uncuffing Kira, I handed her a knife. She had to be quick before the bots killed him. Jason had them trained. It was really impressive. I saw some of his trial runs. Those things were vicious.

Kira grabbed the knife and plunged it into Carlos' stomach. No hesitation. Then she turned the knife and shoved it deeper. "That's for my Mom."

Blood poured from his mouth. He sputtered as if trying to speak. Jason let go of him and whistled to his bots. They scurried away and went back into their case in his pocket.

A servant with a mop came over and started mopping up the blood before Carlos even hit the ground. "His office is at the top of the stairs. Please destroy those bots," she said to Jason.

"I will." He smiled at her. She must have known what they were capable of.

Kira turned to me. Tears filled her eyes. "Thank you."

Derek flung his arm around her. "Come on, Killer. Let's go home."

## CHAPTER 21

## Kira and the shower

CARLOS' BLOOD WAS STILL ON MY HANDS WHEN WE got home. I was shaking while staring at the shower. I killed him. Yes, he absolutely deserved it, but did I have a right to do it? I didn't know.

I turned on the hot water and stepped in. The Triplets had some things to take care of so I was left alone. Maybe a shower would help.

The door opened. All three men walked in. Aiden tossed the shower curtain back.

"I'm fine," I placed my hand on my hip. The water ran down my body. I was exposed to all three of them.

"Yes you are," Derek smirked. He stepped into the shower. His gray sweatpants clung to him exposing his best feature.

"Now spread your legs like a good girl so I can wash you," Aiden demanded.

Maybe this is exactly what I needed. I spread my legs. Derek squirted body wash onto Aiden's hand. Aiden rubbed his hand against my center. The soap slid between my slit. His fingers grazed me.

Jason dropped his pants and shirt. He was already hard

and so fucking big. As Aiden rubbed me Jason entered the shower as well.

Derek was on one side of me and Jason was on the other. Aiden was still standing outside of the shower as he fingered me.

The other two men lathered their hands with soap as well. Jason had shampoo and was massaging my scalp. Derek was concentrating on my tits. All of their hands on me sent me into a dizzy spell. Sweat dripped down my skin, or that was more water, I couldn't tell. My body was on fire.

My pussy dripped onto Aiden's hands. I wanted so badly to cum. I needed to.

Thoughts of Carlos popped into my head. So much blood. The knife twisted into his side so easily. He coughed up blood, some splattered against my face. What had I done?

"Hey!" one of them yelled.

*Yes, he killed my mother but, did that give me a right? Maybe I shouldn't have killed him. Did I make things harder for my men? They would have to cover this up. My stomach turned.*

A hand wrapped around my throat and slammed me into the wall. Not hard, but enough to shake me. I blinked. Aiden was in the shower. He was still in his suit.

"Huh?" I blinked again.

"Get out of your head, Baby." Aiden kept his hand around my throat. "He deserved what happened. Don't make me regret letting you kill him."

"Sorry, I just." I shook my head.

"Now let's get you cleaned up." Derek pulled me toward the shower head.

I let the water run over me. Derek rinsed the soap off of me. Jason moved behind me wrapping his arms around my waist. He kissed my shoulders.

"Time for the back," he whispered into my ear.

Jason pressed my tits against the cold tile. Warm water ran down my back. His hands covered in soap slid across my skin.

I gasped giving into his touch. Forgetting everything else.

"You like that?" He pressed his body into mine. His dick slid between my legs.

"Fuck," I moaned.

Jason grabbed me and lifted me up. He turned me and handed me to Aiden, who was out of the shower.

"Where are you taking me?" I wrapped my arms around his neck.

"The bed and then all three of us are gonna take you over and over." Aiden pressed his lips to mine.

Kissing him took away any other thoughts. I wanted him, needed him. Shit, I needed all three of them.

He placed me on the bed. His kisses trailed down my neck. Derek joined and kissed my tits. He sucked my left nipple and Aiden grabbed the other between his teeth.

Jason climbed onto the bed and placed his dick at my entrance. He slid it up and down, coating it with my juices.

"Wait, condoms," I gasped.

Aiden stopped and stared at me. Fury flashed across his face. "Did you not understand that you are ours?"

"Right, but what if I get pregnant?" I averted my eyes.

"You think what? We won't fuck you when you have a big beautiful belly?" Derek grazed my nipple with his teeth.

"No, it's not that. It's...um..." I tried to find the words to explain it to them.

Jason slid his cock inside me. "Baby, don't you want my cum?"

"Yes," I moaned.

Aiden and Derek went back to sucking my nipples. Jason slid his cock in and out. I wanted more of them, this wasn't enough. I grabbed Derek and pulled him toward me. As he crawled up the bed I grabbed his dick.

Using his dick I guided him further up the bed. Finally I got him to my mouth. I wrapped my lips around his cock. He knew what I wanted and started fucking my mouth.

There was no way I was leaving Aiden out of this. I reached my hand down and realized he was still in his suit. And soaking wet. I pushed Derek out of my mouth for a second. "Take off your clothes," I demanded.

He actually listened. He returned to the bed and I assumed he was completely naked. I couldn't tell because Jason was fucking my pussy and Derek was fucking my mouth.

I reached my hand out again, reaching for Aiden. My hand found his chest so I trailed it down to his cock. I wrapped my hand around it and began jerking him off.

All three of them moaned as I pleased them and they pleased me. I was floating. This was everything. My heart raced, my body was on fire. I never wanted this to end.

Jason took his time going slow and deep. Vibrations crawled through my body. I was getting close to the edge. My moans were muffled by Derek's cock. I bucked against Jason.

"That's it. Cum for my brother." Aiden massaged my breasts.

His words undid me. I came hard. My legs shook. I gasped so hard, I pulled Derek's cock deeper into my throat. He growled.

After that they took turns fucking me. When one wasn't sliding their cock into my pussy, one was in my mouth. The third cock I kept tightly around my hand when I could.

Derek bent me over the bed and fucked me from behind. He grabbed my shoulders and fucked me hard and deep. He groaned each time his dick was fully inside me. Jason and Aiden sat on the bed watching. My pussy dripped.

Aiden had me ride him while his brothers pushed me

deeper onto him. I rolled my hips and slid up and down his cock. His hands grabbed my hips. Fuck, this was all so hot.

"You are a good girl aren't you," Aiden moaned.

I nodded and kept riding.

"Say it," he demanded.

"I'm a good girl," I whispered.

"Louder!" he growled.

"I'm a good girl!" I screamed.

"Yes you are." Derek grabbed my throat. "Now keep fucking my brother."

Jason kissed my back while I rode Aiden. Derek stroked himself while he watched.

They were identical, but I was learning to tell them apart. Especially when they were naked. Each one of them had massive cocks, but they were slightly different. Aiden's was the widest hitting my walls when he was inside me. Derek was the longest, making me feel like he would break through at any moment. Jason had a slight curve that caressed my pussy as he entered me. I loved all of them.

Jason pulled me off of Aiden and put me on the floor. Then he grabbed me and lifted me into the air. I wrapped my legs around him. With one hand on my ass he slid his dick in me. He moved me up and down on his dick. Then his lips found mine and he kissed me.

"Your pussy is so tight," Jason moaned against my lips.

"Well, I was a virgin till you guys." *Might as well tell them.*

"Then how did you know how to fuck?" Derek asked.

"I didn't." I looked back at him.

"Even more reason you are ours." Aiden pulled me off of Jason and placed me on the bed. Guess he wanted his turn.

They had me in so many positions I couldn't tell where they ended and I began. Every inch of my body was kissed. Every part of me was caressed. All of me was loved.

Derek grabbed me again and tossed me on my back. He

rammed his cock into me hard and fast. The other two watched. Sweat dripped. He grabbed my hair and pushed deeper inside.

His cock pulsated. "Fuck," he growled as he came inside me.

Next Jason took his place. He bent my legs up and slid inside of me. "Ready for my cum?"

"Yes," I moaned.

He fucked me slow and gentle. Getting deeper each time. When his cock pulsated I wrapped my legs around him to push him in deeper. Jason ground his teeth as he released himself.

Aiden was last. He pulled one of my legs up and kept the other down. Going at an angle he slid his dick into me. His hand found my throat as he fucked me hard. I grabbed at his back. Nails digging into him.

He continued to slide his cock in and out. There was so much anger in fucking. It was like he was releasing all of that on me. Giving me pleasure to get rid of what anger he held.

I pushed my hips against him. We kept a rhythm going. Each of us giving it all to the other.

"Tell me you want our baby," he purred.

"I want a baby." I grabbed his hair. "I want you guys to give me a baby."

His cock pulsated. My pussy vibrated. I was getting close and so was he. I moaned.

"Cum with me." He took his hand and caressed my face.

My body tingled. I was flying. This was everything. He was taking me closer. Shit, they all did. My men gave me everything I needed. With each stroke of his cock I got closer. I couldn't catch my breath, not that it mattered. Air was meaningless, only they mattered.

Aiden pushed deeper. I flew off the edge. My pussy

pulsated with his cock. He released his load into me. We hit the edge at the same time.

I flopped against the bed.

"You guys are gonna have to rotate who sleeps in bed with me. You can't fuck me and leave me here alone." I wiped my hair from my face.

"Done," they said simultaneously.

"Time for another shower." Aiden lifted me up. "We gotta clean you up."

"There's something else." I bit my lip.

They all looked at me, waiting.

"I love you guys," I blurted. It wasn't easy for me to say. I had never loved anyone except my mother and Vickie. That was different. Loving these three was different.

"I love you." Jason grabbed me and kissed me on the lips.

"Babe, you know I love you." Derek kissed me as well.

"Come on, you need a shower." Aiden walked toward the bathroom.

My heart dropped. He didn't love me. He cared, but not enough. I knew Aiden had a rough exterior, but I didn't realize how rough until now.

Aiden turned to me. A huge smile spread across his face. "I love you too. Never forget that."

# Epilogue The Triplets and The Blonde

I CLIMBED OUT OF THE BED. IT WASN'T EASY, especially since they bought me a much larger bed a few months ago. Since they rotated what nights they slept with me they wanted the best. At least that was my reasoning for the extravagance.

My pink fuzzy slippers and matching robe were right next to the bed. There was no time to find something else. I wrapped the robe around me and left the room. Pat would be showing up with my breakfast soon. I should wait for it. Nope. That was a bad idea.

Every morning my men had a meeting in Aiden's office, it was the perfect place to find all three of them.

"Mrs. Cartright, can I get you something?" Jamal asked as soon as I opened my door.

It wasn't even official yet. Our wedding wasn't for another few months, but that didn't stop the staff from calling me that. I smiled, it was nice to hear.

"Ma'am you really shouldn't." Jamal reached out his hand.

"Oh stop it." I swatted his hand away.

When I entered Aiden's office all three of them were busy looking over some papers on his desk. They stopped when they heard the door shut.

"Hey guys, I gotta..." I started saying.

"Perfect, you're here." Jason came over and kissed me on the lips.

"Come on Babe you gotta see this." Derek guided me over to the desk.

It was blue prints for something. Even though real estate and such was their business, I never saw any interest in it. I spent most of my time feeding the homeless and trying to find them jobs. The Trips let me spend what money I wanted on them as long as it was within reason. I kept pushing each time and so far they hadn't said anything to me about it.

"See?" Aiden pointed to the top.

Kira Heights was written across the top in big bold letters.

"What is this?" I traced my fingers across the letters.

"An apartment complex. This one is for forty apartments." Derek waved his hands at the paper.

"I don't get it. Rich and Elite don't live in apartments." I scrunched up my face. "Not to mention the homeless can't afford it."

"That's why we aren't charging them. When the economy changed apartments were either destroyed or abandoned. Not anymore. This will be the first of many." Aiden smirked.

I wrapped my arms around him and squeezed. "This is perfect. I love you gu...ahhh."

All three surrounded me. "What's wrong?"

"My water," I grunted.

"Oh, you need water?" Derek turned toward the door. "Pat!"

"No, no." I grabbed my stomach. "My water broke."

"Really?" Aiden paled.

I nodded grunting through another contraction.

Jason flipped open his phone just as Pat rushed into the room. He shut the phone. "Perfect timing. Pat, can you get the doctor? The twins are coming."

# Note from the Author

I can't begin to express my love for everyone who has read this book. Thank you so much for supporting me on this journey. Seriously, I am so lucky to have you all in my life. Without all my readers this would be nothing.

When I went to my husband and told him I wanted to write a book with multiple love interests he said 'let's do it.' We had so much fun with this book. I hope you had just as much fun reading it.

Now, I am working on the next book **Bought By Three Men**. If you are interested in teasers check out any of my social media pages.

Till Next Time. Muah,
Callie Sky

facebook.com/authorcalliesky
instagram.com/authorcalliesky
tiktok.com/@authorcalliesky
youtube.com/@calliesky643

## Also by Callie Sky

Bought By Three Men

40672277R00102